## "I need a hug
anything in th

No sooner had Vanessa o...
words than Taylor drew her to him and
held her tight against his chest. After
seeing the ghost last night, she needed the
comfort of another human being. "Do you
kiss as good as you hug?" she asked.

"Better." He grinned cockily and then
proved it. "I was considering seducing you
before you sprang that ghost on me."

Vanessa pulled away reluctantly. "You
can't seduce a woman with a ghost in her
tree."

"Is that a hard-and-fast rule?"

"I don't know." She tried to smile. "This is
my first ghost."

"Mine too – and I'll be damned if I'll let it
come between me and the woman I want."

Dear Reader,

We all have childhood memories of hearing hair-raising stories late at night. Those tales hinted at passions and intrigues beyond our youthful understanding. Glenda Sanders's *Dark Secrets* begins where those spine-tinglers left off. This is a good old-fashioned ghost story—for adults.

I should like to hear your comments on Glenda Sanders's *Dark Secrets*. Please take the time to write to me at the address below.

The Editor
Mills & Boon Temptation
Eton House
18-24 Paradise Road
Richmond
Surrey
TW9 1SR

# *Dark Secrets*

## GLENDA SANDERS

MILLS & BOON LIMITED
ETON HOUSE, 18-24 PARADISE ROAD
RICHMOND, SURREY TW9 1SR

*First published in Great Britain in 1991 by Mills & Boon Limited, Eton House, 18-24 Paradise Road, Richmond, Surrey TW9 1SR*

© Glenda Sanders Kachelmeier 1990

ISBN 0 263 77286 1

21 – 9104

*Made and printed in Great Britain*

# 1

TALONS OF TERROR gripped Vanessa Wiggins in a hold that was inescapable. She writhed and tossed in her sleep, tangling the sheets, twisting them around her. Then, reflexively, she panicked and struggled against the binding folds of fabric.

She awoke instantly, gasping, with none of the grogginess of half sleep. Her senses tingled with unnatural alertness. At once she was aware of the clamminess of the designer bedding and the cool, damp darkness of predawn.

A scream pierced the still air and scraped over her nerve endings—a woman's scream, shrill and discordant, an involuntary screech of raw terror permeated with the knowledge of mortal peril. It must have been a similar scream that had awakened her. Vanessa froze as the awful, soulful sound rent the air again, then faded into a pitiful wail.

The silence that followed was as desolate as that of a tomb.

Scarcely breathing, Vanessa crept out of bed and tiptoed through the blackness to the window. She could barely distinguish the shape of the old oak tree silhouetted by the glow of a distant street lamp. Nothing else was discernible in the stingy light of the new moon, nothing alive or moving. But someone had been there. She was certain of it. The screams had been real.

Someone needed help. A woman was in trouble. Desperate trouble. With trembling fingers, Vanessa dialed 911, then drummed her fingertips on the bedside table until there was an answer. A voice listened to her story, asked her to spell her name and took directions to her house.

Vanessa glanced at the clock. Three-forty. She walked the floor a few minutes, then put on a robe and slippers and brushed her hair and walked the floor some more. Almost half an hour passed before she heard the sound of a car engine outside. Seconds later the doorbell chimed and a deep voice announced, "Sheriff's deputy."

"Mrs. Wiggins?" the uniformed officer asked as she opened the door.

"Miss," she said, stepping aside for him to enter.

He listened to the same story she'd told the voice on the telephone. Skepticism was written on every feature of his face as he jotted notes on a clipboard. "Where did you say this screaming was coming from?" he asked.

"My backyard. It sounded like it was just outside my window. I suppose it could have been one of the neighboring yards." A new thought occurred to her, an unsettling one. "The house behind me is still under construction. You don't think someone could have dragged her in there?"

"I'll check it out."

Through the window, she watched the beam from the deputy's flashlight crisscross the backyard from house to fence and back. It disappeared as he opened the gate, then played peekaboo through the spaces between the slats of the fence as he followed the sidewalk to the vacant house behind hers. She lost track of it until the light splayed through the fence from the adjoining yard.

A shiver passed through her, and she found she was hugging herself against a chill. There was a definite draft near the living room window. When she crossed the room, it was much warmer near the window in the breakfast nook. For almost a minute she couldn't find the deputy's light, but she spied it, finally, coming from the direction of the sidewalk. She opened the back door when she heard the gate latch clink and the telltale squeak of the gate opening.

The deputy shook his head in response to the questioning look on her face. "Nothing amiss," he said, and followed her into the house.

"The vacant house?" she asked.

"It was wide open. I went through every room. Nothing out of the ordinary."

Vanessa wiped her hand over her face. "Someone needed help. I should have—"

"There was no trace of a struggle or any sign that anyone's been here, ma'am."

"But I heard . . ."

The deputy didn't seem to attach much significance to what she'd heard. "These houses are new, aren't they?"

"Yes."

"Have you lived here long?"

She shook her head. "I just moved in."

"You live here alone?"

"Yes."

"Have you ever lived alone before, Miss Wiggins?"

Grasping the gist of his questions, she frowned. "Yes, I have," she said irritably.

"You know, ma'am, every house sounds a little different at night. A new house settles."

"What I heard was not a house settling."

"There are wolves in the lot across the road. They howl sometimes. They can sound pretty human."

"I know the difference between a human scream and a wolf baying at the moon."

The deputy shrugged under her glower. "I didn't find anything out of order. Could have been a cat in heat. We get calls on them from time to time. They sound pretty human."

"Well, thanks for coming, anyway."

The deputy missed the edge of sarcasm in her voice and shrugged again. "Just doing my job."

Arrogant, insensitive chauvinist! Vanessa thought as she clicked the dead bolt into place after he'd gone. He might as well have called her a hysterical broad. His attitude certainly had. All she'd needed after being wrested from sleep by a bloodcurdling scream was some chauvinistic clown telling her what she'd heard was a wolf howling or some lonesome cat.

The mantel clock chimed. Four-thirty. Too early to dress for the day, too late to get any real sleep. Still, she went back to bed and made the effort.

She couldn't gauge how long she took to fall asleep, but it seemed a long time, and when the sun peering through the east windows jolted her awake, she felt as though she hadn't slept at all. Groaning, she rolled over onto her side so that her back was to the light and stole another hour and a half of fitful sleep.

The unsettling experience left her enervated all day. She read the Sunday paper, clipped the coupons in the slick advertising supplements and watched a mediocre movie on television. In midafternoon she dragged herself off the couch, put on jeans and a T-shirt and did the minimum that had to be done to her face and hair before she felt presentable in public.

She went to the plant nursery and the supermarket and brought home three rosebushes, two variegated ligustrums, a bag of bark mulch, a pint of deli clam chowder, a hunk of Muenster cheese and three apples. After putting the groceries away, she set about planting the shrubs and was working up a respectable sweat in the afternoon sun when she heard a deep voice call a greeting.

Taylor Stephenson, immaculate in white jogging shorts and a matching knit tank top, was standing on her sidewalk—or at least, the sidewalk in front of her house. Technically, it was probably his sidewalk, since he owned the development company that had conceived the subdivision.

He looked, she thought, exactly like a wunderkind entrepreneur, which was exactly what he was. Speculating on Houston's expansion into the isolated rural communities, he'd turned what had once been a farm area known as Wolf Corner into a suburban paradise for young, upwardly mobile professionals. He was an idealist and a democratic one: he lived in the neighborhood he'd dreamed up and then turned into reality. The big house on the large cul-de-sac lot at the end of Bay-at-the-Moon Lane was his. Vanessa lived a block away, at the corner of Bay-at-the-Moon and Howling Wolf Drive.

Smiling, resplendent in the sunshine with the light haloing his cap of golden brown hair, Taylor walked toward her. "Doing a little gardening?"

Vanessa was a mature woman of twenty-six. She managed not to swoon under the effect of that devastating smile and returned it, instead. "Very little. I've done some pruning and mowing, but I've never done much planting. Do you know how much mulch you're supposed to mix with this soil?"

"What you're doing looks about right. Then use all mulch for the top few inches." Taking the shovel from her hand, he said, "Here, let me give you a hand."

"It's really not necessary, Mr. Stephenson. I can . . ."

His grin was endearing. Almost genuine. As if he were just an overgrown all-American boy instead of a paragon of eligible bachelorhood. "I promise you the feminist movement won't crumble if you let a man do some of the manual labor. And call me Taylor. We're neighbors."

"Well, *Taylor*, would it sound militant if I point out that you're going to get all dirty?"

"I was getting ready to jog, anyway. It'll be a good warm-up." The flat shovel landed with a series of dull thunks as he packed mulch around the ligustrum. "Where to from here?"

Vanessa selected a spot for the next ligustrum, and he drove in the shovel. Imagine! The wunderkind planting shrubs in her yard.

With measured nonchalance, he said, "I ran into a couple of deputies at the donut shop this morning. Understand you had a little excitement last night."

*So that's what he's doing here.* Vanessa tried not to be disappointed. "Excitement is not the word for it," she said. "I was terrified." She put her hand on her waist and took an aggressive stance. "Look, I know the cop probably made me sound like some hysterical heroine from a nineteenth-century Gothic novel, but what I heard wasn't a wolf."

Taylor stood the shovel in the soil and crossed his arms over the handle. "I wouldn't think so. Not close to the window. They pretty much stay in the underbrush."

Vanessa exhaled heavily. "I can't shake the feeling that there's a woman lying dead or injured somewhere. Do you suppose the sheriff's department would notify me if they found one?"

"I doubt it," he said flatly. "They'd be more likely to tell me in a confidential whisper."

Vanessa frowned. Of course they would. The entire situation clarified in her mind like a slide being focused on a screen. A discreet phone call. *Thought you might want to know about this, since it's in your subdivision.* Taylor Stephenson was troubleshooting, not flirting.

"I don't think anyone's going to find a murdered woman," he assured her.

"Don't keep me in suspense," she said sharply. "If not a wolf or a woman, what *do* you think I heard?"

"A peacock," he said. "Or, more accurately, a peahen. From the Lost Horizon Restaurant. It's only about half a mile from us, cross-country. We had trouble with them from time to time when we were clearing the land. Gave our crew a real spook the first time. They sound exactly like a woman. Far more human than a wolf's cry. It could have been next to your window one minute and gone without a trace the next."

"That's more credible than the wolf theory," she admitted grudgingly.

"But you're not convinced."

"If the deputies found a body and told you, would you tell me?"

Taylor drove the shovel into the soil and scooped up a clump of dirt, then cocked an eyebrow at her. "Are you sure you'd want to know?"

"I wish I could believe that what I heard *was* a peahen."

The shovel bit into the earth again; another scoop of dirt was tossed aside. Taylor inverted the plastic pot that held the ligustrum and positioned the shrub in the hole he'd dug. "Hold this straight." Vanessa grabbed the shrub as instructed, and he mixed mulch and soil and packed it around the root ball. "You know," he said, "I could get here a lot quicker from my house than the deputies could from God knows where. I'll give you my number, just in case."

"I couldn't ask you to—"

"Nonsense! What are neighbors for? Besides, if there's a peahen running around terrorizing my home owners, we have to get her crated up and shipped back to the Lost Horizon before she stirs up any more havoc."

Taylor insisted on helping with the rosebushes. He and Vanessa worked efficiently as a team, with a minimum of conversation. When they'd finished, she offered to make coffee or iced tea, but he declined either, anxious to be off for his run.

They said goodbye, but she called his name as he turned toward the sidewalk. He stopped in midstride and looked back at her. She was staring at her foot while she drew imaginary circles on the grass with the toe of her sneaker. Her voice was very low. "I'd rather believe the peahen theory," she said. She lifted her head and tilted it back to look directly at his face. "But I would want to know if they found a body."

He nodded gravely before jogging away.

KAREN LAKE was a year younger than Vanessa and had been teaching sophomore English for two years in the same high school where Vanessa taught history. Friendship had blossomed between the two women as they became acquaintances and, later, confidantes during their free hour every day in the teachers' lounge.

Physically they were quite different. Karen, tall and slender, wore her dark hair in a short bob. Her taste in clothing ran to tailored suits in the classroom, classic shirts and gabardine slacks for casual wear. Vanessa, average in height and more voluptuous in build, preferred clothes with soft lines and jeans and knit tops around the house. Her hair, deep brown with golden highlights, was thick and long.

The two attributed their close friendship to the fact that they were different enough to balance each other out. Whatever the reason, it worked. They chatted in the teachers' lounge, attended mandatory extracurricular activities together and occasionally visited each other's homes. Once or twice Vanessa and her escort of the moment had double-dated with Karen and her husband of less than a year, Bob.

Karen listened to Vanessa's tale of screams, chauvinistic deputies and helpful neighbors, then summed it up succinctly. "So the cop thought it was a wolf or a love-sick cat, and Stephenson thought what you'd heard was a lost peacock?"

"Peahen," Vanessa replied. "Pretty farfetched, isn't it? But then, the idea of a woman screaming her head off outside my window and then disappearing without a trace sounds just as farfetched."

She sighed through a frown. "No wonder Taylor Stephenson came diddlybopping down to make sure I wasn't spreading bad word of mouth about his precious subdivision. For a few glorious moments I actually thought he'd noticed I was a flesh-and-blood woman and not just one of the young, single professionals he's so anxious to get to buy his houses."

"I think the whole bunch of you are way off base," Karen said.

"Regarding?"

"Who or what was outside your window. Vanessa, how dense can you get? You're a schoolteacher. Who would be screaming outside your window on a Saturday night?"

Vanessa cocked her head skeptically. "A student?"

"Who else?"

"I can't believe—"

"More likely a whole group of them. Scaring a teacher senseless probably seemed like a hilarious way to spice up a Saturday night. They probably parked down the street and waited for the cops, giggling and hooting."

Shaking her head, Vanessa said, "I can't believe students could be so cruel."

"Flunk any basketball players lately?"

"Just— It does sound like something Tony Davis would dream up, doesn't it?"

"He probably recruited Heather McQueen to go along as the screamer. That girl has the lungs to supply the sound track for a horror movie. Of course, you'll never know for sure unless they get to bragging about their exploits. Sometimes I wonder why we stay in this profession."

"You wonder that at least twice a week, usually after fourth period," Vanessa said.

"Let's talk about something more pleasant," suggested Karen. "Like the housewarming you're having this weekend. Is everything ready?"

"Just about," Vanessa said, relieved at the change of subject. She was sick of theories about what she'd heard. One thing she was sure of, though: if Heather McQueen was the screamer outside her window, the girl should become an actress; her performance of a terrified woman had been worthy of an Academy Award.

# 2

KAREN AND HER HUSBAND, Bob, were the first to arrive for the housewarming. Bob, tall and husky, came in looking like a nineteenth-century dockworker, with a bag of ice slung over each shoulder. "Point me toward an ice chest," he said, exaggerating a shiver. "This ice is f-freezing."

"On the floor, across from the fridge," Vanessa directed. She took the tray of hors d'oeuvres Karen had brought and put it on the white-clothed table in the breakfast nook. "Margaret's bringing some kind of centerpiece for the table from her yard," she said, referring to the chairman of the history department. "I hope she gets here a little ahead of the others. The table looks so naked."

"Did I hear someone say naked?" Bob said, emerging from the kitchen. "Are we getting naughty already?"

"One-track mind," said Karen, rolling her eyes.

"Yes, yes, yes," he said lasciviously, grasping her from behind and smooching her neck. Karen laughed, tried to twist away from him and nearly lost her balance. Bob grabbed her and planted noisy stage kisses on her nape.

Smiling, Vanessa cleared her throat—a schoolteacher's gesture. Karen forced a serious face and straightened her clothes. "Behave yourself, Bob. I promised Vanessa I'd help." Then, to Vanessa, she said, "Put us to work. Muscles here does manual labor and I do anything cerebral."

"I need someone to light candles. Is that brains or brawn?"

Karen planted two open hands against Bob's back and shoved him toward the couch. "Sit down, big boy. We'll handle this one."

"Light any wick you can find," Vanessa said, tossing Karen a box of matches. "Start at the mantel and work toward the window. I'll get the sideboard."

"Hey," Karen said a few minutes later, "did you know you have a draft in this corner?"

Vanessa had progressed from the sideboard to the sconces on the breakfast nook wall. She looked at Karen. "I thought that corner seemed chilly the other night."

"The candle keeps going out. Watch." Karen lit the candle in question. The wick caught flame, the flame danced wildly, then faded into a trail of smoke. "I've tried five or six times."

"Pretty substantial draft," Bob observed.

"Stephensco customer service will hear about it," Vanessa said.

"Speaking of Stephensco, what did you decide about inviting Taylor Stephenson to the party tonight?"

"I was going to invite him if I happened to see him again, but I haven't seen him, so . . ." Dismissing the subject of Taylor Stephenson, she regarded the unlit candle with irritation. "That corner needs a spot of light." She lifted a hurricane lamp from the sideboard. "Would this look all right there, or do you think it's too big?"

"Try it," Karen urged.

"Looks fine to me," Bob said from the couch when the lamp was in place.

"To me, too," Karen agreed, admiring the lamp. "Is it an antique?"

"I haven't had it dated," Vanessa answered. "I found it in the old bunkhouse at Grandma Wiggins's farm."

The doorbell rang, and Vanessa opened the door to face two aromatic masses of purple and pink blossoms. "Margaret," she exclaimed, stepping back to make room for the older woman to enter. "Roses. And wisteria. They're gorgeous. Look, Karen, she brought wisteria. Can you smell it over there?"

"Oh, yes," Karen said, "like grapes—" She stopped abruptly, her eyes fixed on the vases of flowers. The color drained from her face slowly, leaving it bloodlessly pale as her smile waned and her jaw dropped open, slack. A tremor passed visibly through her body.

Bob leaped off the sofa, calling her name. As he embraced her, she put her hand to her forehead and shook her head jerkily from side to side, sluffing off the daze that had enveloped her. Color rushed back into her face like red wine poured into a crystal goblet.

Still pressing her fingers to her temple, Karen looked at the trio of concerned faces staring at her. "I...I'm all right," she stammered. "I just felt . . . I don't know . . . peculiar . . . for a moment. Have you ever heard the expression, 'Someone walked over my grave'? It was that sort of feeling." She laughed softly. "Listen to me. How macabre can one get?"

"Maybe you're pregnant," Margaret teased, but the attempted humor fell on fallow soil.

"I think she got chilled," Bob said.

"Get her out of that draft," Vanessa said. "Why don't you lie down on the couch, Karen."

Bob guided her to the couch and sat on the edge beside her, holding her hand.

From the corner of her eye, Vanessa caught sight of Margaret shifting uncomfortably, still holding the pots of flowers. "Oh, Margaret, I didn't mean to leave you standing there with both hands full. Let me take one of those vases. The wisteria will be perfect on the dining table, and you can put the roses there on the end table. Maybe the draft will keep them fresh."

Vanessa stepped back to admire the table. Purple wisteria blossoms draped over the edges of a plump vase to brush the contrasting white of the tablecloth, and tendrils of the wisteria vine reached out from the arrangement like wild, greedy fingers. "It *is* perfect," she told Margaret. "I adore wisteria."

"I got the cutting for that vine years ago from my mother's yard," Margaret said. "I nursed it from a twig, and now it's threatening to swallow my house!" She turned to Vanessa. "I brought you some cuttings I rooted. They're in the trunk of the car, in coffee cans. Nothing fancy, but I wanted to tell you about them since you'll be opening presents later and I couldn't wrap mine."

"What a thoughtful gift," Vanessa said. "I've been wanting something for a spot of color in the yard. Would wisteria vine over a fence?"

She didn't get an answer because the doorbell rang again.

This time it was Father Joe Rogers, the minister of Faith Memorial. Father Joe was a cherub of a man. Everything about him seemed slightly round: the top of his balding head, his chipmunk cheeks, his stubby fingers, his protruding tummy gone soft with rich diet and his pear-shaped behind widened from sitting as he prepared sermons or counseled his flock.

Vanessa wasn't officially a member of the Faith Memorial congregation, but she had attended a few services with Karen and Bob and had been included in various events planned by the young adults of the church. So Karen had insisted that Father Joe perform a traditional house blessing ceremony in Vanessa's new home, and it was for this reason he had come to the housewarming celebration.

Chuckling jubilantly, he poked a football-shaped parcel at Vanessa as he entered. "Our youngest son came down with a bug, so Sylvia insisted on staying home with him, but she made this bread for the ceremony."

The towel-wrapped loaf was still warm and redolent with the scent of yeast. "How thoughtful of her," Vanessa said. "I'll put it in the kitchen for the time being. I'm sorry your son's ill."

"Just a bug," Father Joe assured her.

Again, the doorbell precluded conversation, and it rang persistently as the guests arrived—teachers from school, young people from the church, former neighbors. They listened respectfully as Father Joe conducted the house blessing; they prayed together; they shared the loaf of homemade bread and passed the communal wine; they held hands and sang "Blest Be the Tie that Binds."

Afterward, they ate and drank, chatting and laughing. Vanessa, wearing a frontier-style chambray dress and one long, fat braid slung over her shoulder, relished her role of gracious hostess. She scurried around replenishing ice buckets and talking to her friends, glowing as they heaped praise on her home.

"I understand you were lucky enough to get a tree," Father Joe said. He had followed Vanessa into the kitchen, where she was wrapping the bread left over from the ceremony.

"It's an oak," Vanessa answered. "I had to pay a five-hundred-dollar premium for it, but since my down payment for this house came from my share of my grandfather's insurance money, it seemed fitting. He was a man of the soil. I think he'd have wanted me to have a tree."

"A fitting memorial to him," Father Joe agreed.

"I'd like to get a porch swing like the one in the front yard of the rectory, but I'm not sure the lowest limb is straight enough for one to hang properly."

"Would you like me to take a look at it?" Father Joe said. "I've hung that swing at three rectories. I should be something of an expert on tree limbs."

"I'd love an expert opinion," she said. "You could take a look at it now. I was just about to carry out some of this trash." She grinned at him. "My plastic bag runneth over."

Father Joe carried the bulging bag outside. After they had succeeded in stuffing it into the metal can in the corner of the yard, they walked toward the old oak. Vanessa pointed to the limb she thought most suited to mounting a swing.

Father Joe nodded thoughtfully. "Yes. It looks straight enough—"

The two of them froze in place. Inside, the stereo belched music, and Vanessa's friends and co-workers chatted and drank and ate and laughed together. But outside an eerie silence descended. The air suddenly grew heavy and dank. Vanessa forgot to breathe as she stared, disbelieving, at the figure dangling from the tree limb that had been bare seconds before. It was—or appeared to have once been—a man, and it was hanging by the neck at the end of a rope. From somewhere a breeze blew across the specter, stirring it. Its head wobbled limply and resettled at a grotesque angle.

Vanessa's sharp gasp was the only sound courageous enough to disrupt the dreadful silence. Mesmerized by the pathetic hanging figure, drawn by it, she stepped closer to the tree. That was when she saw the face, a horrible, repulsive, hollow face distorted by agony.

She wanted to look away but could not. She could only stand, motionless, and watch shriveled eyelids open to reveal empty black sockets; could only stare, transfixed, while shriveled lips moved as though trying to speak. Revulsion raised bile in her throat, yet Vanessa did not feel fear, only an overwhelming sense of compassion for the hideous figure, an inexplicable need to alleviate the pathetic figure's suffering.

She raised her arm, extending it toward the apparition, and might have moved forward to touch the figure hanging from the tree limb if Father Joe had not touched her at that moment.

The instant Father Joe's quelling hand landed on her shoulder, the phantom disappeared.

In the distance, the piercing wail of a baying wolf knifed through the stillness of night with the violence of a dropping guillotine blade.

To Vanessa and Father Joe, sensibilities returned slowly. Reason, but not tranquillity. Vanessa was unaware that she was crying, but the tracks of tears were fresh on her cheeks. "You saw it, too?" she asked tremulously.

Father Joe's characteristic joviality had disintegrated; he looked strangely old and abysmally worn-out. A pallor had claimed his normally pink face, and his voice was a mere whisper. "I saw."

"What? H-how?"

"I don't know." Cradling his head in his hands, he shook it slowly back and forth and repeated the phrase several times in a thin, hopeless voice. Vanessa wondered briefly if he might burst into tears.

"He needed help," she said, and turned large eyes on Father Joe's face. "Did you feel it, too? He was asking for help."

"It wasn't—couldn't have been—real. He . . . it . . . existed only in our minds."

Vanessa was hugging herself; she felt cold and nauseated. "It was so real. The face . . . that horrible, tortured face."

"No," he said sharply. "It wasn't real, and we mustn't yield to the temptation to believe it was."

"But . . ."

He was stern, almost fanatical. "It couldn't have been real."

"If it . . . he . . . wasn't real, then why did we both see it at the same time?"

Grasping her shoulders, he said urgently, "Vanessa, we mustn't discuss this with anyone. It could be—probably is—some cruel practical joke. We can't say anything about it until we learn what we're dealing with."

Sensing the desperation in his plea, she drew in a ragged breath and forced herself to stop shaking. "Okay. All right," she said, patronizing him. "It makes sense to wait."

For several minutes they stood facing each other, but neither of them spoke. Then Father Joe said simply, "We have to go inside."

Blotting her eyes with her fingertips, Vanessa nodded. "You're not feeling faint?" he asked.

"I'm okay," she said tautly, not feeling that way at all.

In the house, she forced a fixed smile on her face and walked straight to the bathroom adjacent to her bedroom. The damage to her makeup was not as severe as she might have imagined. She pressed a damp cloth to her face and held it there a moment, then removed a few smudges of mascara with a cotton swab and applied a fresh coat to her lashes.

Smiling her way back through the living room, she entered the kitchen, poured herself a glass of wine, downed it in a single gulp, poured herself another glass and began circulating among her guests again. She appeared the perfect hostess, but her friendly smile and solicitous manner were a thin veneer that covered near panic.

Father Joe was the first to leave. "I promised Sylvia I'd be home early," he said. "Church in the morning, you know." In a discreet whisper, he said, "I'll be back tomorrow around two."

The choir director from the school had fetched a guitar from his car and was getting ready to lead a sing-along. Vanessa joined her guests, settling Indian-style on the floor with the full skirt of her dress draped over her knees. Only a whisper of sound escaped her tight throat as she mouthed the songs everyone else was singing, but no one seemed to notice.

It was past one before the party broke up. Vanessa fell victim to a fresh wave of nervous reaction as soon as the last guest was shuttled out the door. Sleep, she knew, would be impossible, so she filled the tub with hot water and soaked for an hour, crying, trembling, suppressing the urge to scream.

After finishing off a bottle of wine that had been opened at the party, she still did not feel as though she could sleep. The image of that horrible, pitiful face was too fresh in her mind. Impulsively she opened the blinds in her bedroom window just enough to enable her to see the giant oak as she lay in her bed.

She stared at it until dawn, but all she saw were gnarled branches swaying peacefully in the occasional light breeze.

*Cropville, Texas—1945*

THE WHISPER of fine black net on Jessica Vandover's hat strained against her forehead in the breeze as she sat on the review platform waiting for the victory parade. In her tweed suit, crisp white blouse and black grosgrain ribbon tie, she looked as staid as the fellow dignitaries surrounding her. The portly mayor on her left and the strapping sheriff on her right dwarfed her, but in the three years since her father's death, Jessica had ceased feeling self-conscious about being the smallest, youngest and only female among Cropville's ruling elite.

Jon Erick Vandover had left her a two-story house, an automobile, several productive oil wells and the presidency of the Cropville Farmers Bank and Trust: financial security, social standing and God-like power in this small farming community. But the blessings of her birthright were not without price. As she sat on her thronelike chair, Jessica felt strangely detached from the merrymaking, the tinny marches being played by the

high school band and the thronging mass of Cropville
citizens celebrating the end of World War II.

With a twinge of envy, Jessica noted that most of the
women her age were hanging possessively on the arms
of returned veterans. She didn't try to deny the envy;
recently she had felt more like an institution than a
person, and she had come to relish her human emotions, the painful as well as the pleasant. She found the
envy oddly reassuring.

Her attention focused on a handsome couple oblivious to anything or anyone except each other. Fleet-
ingly she wondered if Danny Bannerson was home
from France and, if so, what he was doing today and
with whom he was doing it. The one blurry snapshot
she had of her wartime pen pal showed him to be nice
looking, almost handsome.

The mayor took his place behind the flag-draped
podium, but Jessica wasn't listening to the predictable
rhetoric he was spewing about the bravery of the
Cropville native sons who had served their country
valiantly and well. Her mind remained preoccupied
with Danny Bannerson.

There had been a time when she believed that Danny
might be curious enough about her to ferret out Cropville and meet her. Now she acknowledged the whimsy
in that fairy-tale fantasy. The dimples in her cheeks
deepened as she clamped her mouth shut to suppress
self-mocking laughter at the irony of a bank president
entertaining romantic notions about some war hero in
a Marine Corps uniform. Some of her staunch, down-
to-earth depositors would close their accounts in the
face of such foolishness!

# 3

NOT COMING. Father Joe was not coming. Snatches of his explanation, his apology, his excuses, all made by telephone at precisely 2:06, played repeatedly through Vanessa's mind.

*"Must put it out of our minds . . . too controversial . . . the church wouldn't understand . . . my whole career at stake . . . must think of my children . . . so sorry. . . ."*

Vanessa had listened to his rambling monologue unable to believe what she was hearing.

"You're not coming" was all she'd been able to say when the other end of the line suddenly fell silent.

He had cowed to the soft accusation, becoming even more addled. He repeated his excuses, slurring the disjointed phrases. And then, without warning, there was a click, followed by the hum of the dial tone.

Vanessa had continued holding the receiver in her hand, her fingers crushing around the hard plastic with futile force. Then, when she realized what she was doing, she slammed the instrument back on its cradle and buried her face in her hands. A wrenching sigh made its way through her throat. It sounded like a groan of pain. She could feel hysteria poking at her, prodding, clawing, trying to get inside the thin shell of her composure. She was close to tears, but she couldn't let herself cry for fear of losing the last threads of the tenuous control she had on her beleaguered emotions.

If only Father Joe had shown up to help her investigate what they'd seen; if only he had admitted that they had seen something that bore investigation. But he had bailed out on her in the face of crisis. He was denying, demanding that she deny what, in her mind, was undeniable.

*Coward!* she thought. *Coward.*

Exhausted and alone—his betrayal had left her so very alone—she went out into the backyard dominated by the old oak. The majesty of it, its venerable size and age, impressed her anew. Spring sunlight stabbed through the tree's dark, gnarled branches and danced brightly on the surface of its new leaves. She was struck by the peace inherent in its natural beauty, the tranquillity of art created by nature, inimitable by man. Strange, she thought, that her thoughts should be of peace when her emotions were in a state of siege.

She stood under the tree, with the long limb suspended over her head, and looked up at it, searching. For what, she wasn't sure. For rope burns, perhaps, or a notch where a rope might have grown into the bark. Some sign that what she had seen had actually been there. Some proof that she was not on the fringe of madness.

Perhaps Father Joe wasn't a coward. Perhaps they were both mad, and only he clung to enough sanity to turn his back on the madness.

Vanessa groaned miserably. She hadn't the strength for denial, and even in the tranquil, bright beauty of spring sunshine she sensed, deep inside herself, the conviction that the figure in the tree had come to her with a plea for help.

*Just like the woman screaming outside her window.*
Frustration settled over her like a fog. The screaming

woman didn't exist, either. She was a baying wolf or a
peahen or a student, depending on whether Vanessa
chose to listen to the sheriff's deputy, her hotshot developer neighbor or her best friend. But they hadn't
heard the screams, and Vanessa had. *Just as she'd seen
the ghost.*

She laughed, a high-pitched laugh that held a note
of hysteria. A ghost. God! Maybe she should check the
home owner's manual to see how the builder recommended new home owners handle ghosts. But of
course, the ghost came with the tree, and the tree was
not an integral part of the structure, so there was no
warranty on it. No operating instructions. No free ex-
orcisms by customer service. Vanessa laughed again,
the same high-pitched, hysterical sound. Was Ghost-
busters listed in the telephone book?

Someone—or something—knocked at the wooden
gate. Vanessa turned her gaze to the high gate, afraid
to walk over and open it for fear of what she would
find. For fear of finding nothing at all. It was probably
the resident poltergeist out for some Sunday afternoon
jollies.

"Yo?"

Vanessa expelled the breath she hadn't been aware
she was holding and covered her face with her hands.
A human voice if ever she'd heard one. A male voice.
The voice of Taylor Stephenson, if memory served her
correctly. She'd never heard anything more beautiful
in her life.

Taylor hadn't planned on stopping for a visit, but
he'd heard what sounded like laughter and decided to
say hello. The gate swung open, "Yo, yourself," she
greeted him.

"I thought I heard you back here," he replied. "How's it going? Any more middle-of-the-night scares?"

She looked up at his face but didn't answer. Her eyes were blue gray rimmed by indigo. There was a sadness in them that appealed to a protective instinct inside him. Automatically Taylor fought down that instinct. Protecting women was a dangerous proposition in the late twentieth century. Modern women didn't want a man protecting them; old-fashioned women read too much into it when a man did. A man raised either a woman's ire or her expectations for his efforts.

She still had not answered him. He said, "I ran into that deputy again this morning. They haven't found any bodies unaccounted for."

"Good," she said. "I hope they don't. I didn't want—"

"I know."

Her teak and maple hair was braided and hung over her right shoulder, ending just above her breast. The braid, the absence of makeup, her oversize jersey and cutoff jeans all made her seem younger than he knew her to be, which was four years short of thirty.

A teacher. Given a list of five jobs she might have held, he would probably have picked teacher. She possessed a number of qualities that made a good teacher, wholesomeness being predominant among them. Her lack of affectation was the first thing he'd noticed about her. After her eyes.

"Would you like a glass of lemonade?" she asked.

He had an acceptance on his tongue, but she went on before he could reply, as though she were afraid he might turn down her invitation. "I think there's some wine and beer left over from last night."

"Lemonade's fine," he said. And then, because he was curious, he said, "I noticed the cars last night."

Vanessa had walked to the door. She paused with her hand on the knob and looked at him. "It was a house-warming."

"That's nice," he said. "It's a nice custom."

She opened the door and led him inside. It was exactly the kind of room he would have expected, warm and informal. It smelled of flowers, and he noted the bouquet of roses on an end table, the bowl of cut wisteria on the table in the breakfast nook. Vanessa had gone directly to the kitchen. He followed and leaned against the doorjamb, watching as she took glasses from the cabinet and then opened the refrigerator freezer for ice. She filled the glasses, then went back to the refrigerator for the pitcher of lemonade.

Her back was to him. He noticed her well-shaped legs, her rounded hips, and admired them, thinking that he'd like to touch her. The left side of her neck was bare, and he felt a strong urge to kiss her there.

He tried to imagine what it would be like to be in her class, to call her Miss Wiggins and dread one of those down-the-nose reproachful scowls teachers invariably perfect in classroom experience. He succeeded, instead, in imagining what her neck would taste like and then wanted to touch her worse than ever.

She put down the pitcher, braced both hands on the counter and sighed. A tremor passed through her shoulders.

"Vanessa?"

"Please talk to me," she said. "Say something, anything. Just talk to me."

Taylor thought he heard the liquid quality of tears in her voice. He knew he recognized desperation. The instinct to protect her was stronger than ever, and he had to struggle to quell it. He swallowed. What was he supposed to say?

"You've got a great behind, Teacher."

Vanessa let out a short volley of laughter and closed her eyes, sealing back the tears of relief. It was so perfect, so outrageous, so wonderfully silly. So absolutely *normal*.

Taylor's battle with his protective instincts was lost when he saw another tremor in her shoulders, followed by the conscious stiffening of her spine. He stepped behind her and cupped his hand around her neck, slipping his fingers under the heavy braid. Her neck muscles were knotted with tension. "Want to talk about it?" he asked.

Her shoulders sagged and her head bowed forward. He heard her exhale a lungful of air.

"I'm not sure I can," she said.

Her skin was smooth and warm. Woman skin. Taylor didn't want to take his hands off her. But he hadn't anticipated anything like this. He knew enough about women to know that when a woman said she wasn't sure she could talk about something, talking was what she wanted to do more than anything else in the world.

Decision time, he thought. Listen or retreat. March or die. Risk getting involved or get the hell out. With a growl of resignation, he pulled his hand off her neck and went to the refrigerator to forage for the wine she'd mentioned earlier. "Are you saving this for some special occasion?"

She shook her head. Taylor set the wine on the counter and broke the seal to discover a screw-off lid. Ordinarily he would have made some teasing comment, but he simply opened the wine, then rummaged around in the cabinet for a glass. He found a small one and filled it and offered it to Vanessa, lifting her hand and wrapping it around the glass. She tried to smile. "Are you plying me with liquor now that you finally got around to noticing my behind?"

It was a gallant effort at humor, but it fell short because of the halting tension in her voice.

"Strictly medicinal," he said. "I'm trying to loosen you up. Now down with it."

She took a dainty swallow.

"Quit piddling around," he coaxed impatiently. "Down with it."

She cast him a dubious scowl over the rim of the glass. "Aren't you supposed to sip wine?"

"Not in emergency situations."

"Bottoms up, then," she said, and doffed it in one draft.

"Good girl," he said, and refilled the glass. "This one you can sip or chugalug. You call it."

She chugalugged and gave him the glass again. "This time, I'll sip."

He poured more wine into the glass, took her free hand in his and led her into the living room. "Now," he said. "Sit back, relax, and tell Uncle Taylor all about it."

She closed her eyes and sighed. "I don't know where to begin."

None of them ever knew where to begin! Taylor thought. "Relax a few minutes," he said. "Let the wine work. It'll be easier."

He settled into the end of the overstuffed sofa opposite her and hoped, in the deepest depths of his heart, that he wasn't going to hear about a lover incapable of making a commitment or a married man who couldn't leave his wife for the sake of his children. He'd heard more than enough dirty-rotten-bastard stories from women to last him the rest of his life.

It was a curse, being a nice guy and a good listener, having a heart like a marshmallow where women were concerned. They talked, he listened. They thanked him very nicely, said they wished they could find someone half as kind and wonderful and sensitive as he was, then went back to their insensitive jerks and married lovers.

Things had changed, of course, since Stephensco had grown from a fledgling dream into a hot young company. He'd switched from cutoff jeans to silk-blend suits and abandoned the corner barber for trendy styling salons. Women pursued him now, a real turnabout from the old days. But to his dismay, the ones who pursued him were the female counterparts to all the male jerks and losers he'd heard about from women: fortune hunters, status seekers, users. There just weren't enough hours left at the end of a company president's workday to go looking for the kind of woman who cared as much about a man as she did about his end-of-year profits. On those rare evenings that he managed to get home early, he usually fell asleep in front of the television, exhausted from getting up before the sun to touch base with his construction crews, then putting in a full day's work at the Stephensco office.

Vanessa had tilted her head back against the plush cushions on the sofa. Her eyes were closed. He could see the pulse beating in her throat and wanted to taste the soft skin his fingers had touched earlier, to feel that pulse quicken under his tongue. A preemptive warmth gathered in his loins. He'd never seduced a woman in the middle of listening to her problems before, but this woman was capable of making a man rethink policy. No sense being inflexible. He didn't seem to have time for honor anymore, and honor was an anachronous concept, anyway.

She opened her eyes, those big blue eyes haunted by a profound sadness, and took a generous sip of her wine. Her gaze settled on his face. She looked lost and desolate.

"What is it?" he asked. "A man?"

How was she supposed to answer that? Vanessa thought. Her impression of the figure in the tree was that it had been male. But could she call it a man? "I'm not . . . I guess you could say it's a man."

*Oh, no*, Taylor thought. *She's just found out the man she's in love with is gay.* He'd heard that one before, too.

His eyes locked with hers again, and seduction became a viable consideration. It would be so simple. A shoulder to cry on, soothing kisses, healing embraces. Then whispered entreaties. *You're a warm, beautiful woman who's hurting. I'm a sensitive, lonely man who desires you. Let's go to the bedroom and soothe each other.*

It seemed to him that she was reading his thoughts, encouraging him, when she said thinly, "Do you . . ."

The breath caught in his throat as he watched her swallow before starting over. He wasn't prepared for the question that she finally uttered with a shuddering intensity. It was, "Do you believe in ghosts?"

# 4

"GHOSTS?" TAYLOR PARROTED, not quite believing what he'd heard. "You mean clanking chains and heavy footsteps and doors that open and shut by themselves?"

"You're making fun of me," she said miserably, and he watched despair deteriorate into utter desperation in her eyes.

"No, I just . . ."

Her eyes widened with a new realization. "People are going to think I'm crazy." She dealt the padded back of the couch a blow with her balled fist. "Damn it, I can't believe he's such a coward!"

"The ghost?"

"No!" she said. "Father Joe." She dropped her face into her hands and sighed.

"Slow down a little," Taylor said. "Who is Father Joe?"

She lowered her hands but kept her head tucked, staring into her lap. "The minister who conducted the house blessing ceremony last night."

"And why is he a coward?"

"He's the only other witness," she said. "The only other person who saw it. And he's not going to back me up."

She wilted visibly. Taylor put his hand on her sagging shoulder consolingly. "Start at the beginning."

"We went out to look at the oak tree," she said. "I've been thinking about hanging a swing, and since Father Joe hung the one at the rectory, I asked him . . ."

She faltered. He squeezed her shoulder reassuringly. "It's broad daylight, Vanessa. You don't have to be afraid."

"I'm not afraid. It's not fear, it's . . . futility."

Touching her, looking into her eyes, Taylor felt her desperation. He wanted to absorb her, lend her his own strength, his own self-assurance. "You saw a ghost?"

She told him everything, about the hideousness of the withered face with its empty eye sockets, her impression that the specter was appealing to her for help, Father Joe's plea that they investigate the scene by light of day before reaching any conclusions, then his refusal to get involved.

"He says there are only two kinds of power, good and evil, and that if a ghost exists, it comes from evil power. He says we have to turn away from it, because giving it attention grants it more power."

"He saw it, too? You're sure of that?"

"Positive. I might doubt what I'd seen, but we saw the same thing at the same time. I find the idea of simultaneous hallucinations harder to swallow than the idea of a ghost."

After a thoughtful silence, she said, "Father Joe says the issue of ghosts is so controversial he can't afford to go on record as having seen one. He's worried about his standing in the church if he becomes involved, his career. Our ghost or apparition or whatever it was seems to be rather political."

"So he's going to ignore it out of existence."

"That's the game plan. The problem is, it leaves me out in the cold, with no one to corroborate my story."

Her eyes met his, held them in challenge. "Well, you're the first one I've told. Do you think I'm crazy?"

"You've got to admit the story is bizarre. I've never believed in ghosts myself...."

"I don't blame you," she said miserably. "I didn't believe in ghosts, either, until one started hanging around outside. A few days ago, if someone had told me they'd seen what I saw, I'd have thought they were crazy."

Grasping her upper arms for emphasis, he said, "You're perfectly sane, Vanessa."

"Then you believe me? You believe it actually—"

"I believe that you saw something that was very real to you. And apparently, it was too real for comfort to Father Joe."

"If you mean that you don't think I conjured up a ghost to liven up an otherwise dull existence, thank you. You're giving me more credit than the cop who came out to check out the screams last weekend."

"If he thought that, then he's a jerk," Taylor said.

She smiled wryly. "Why the big vote of confidence? You don't know me. I certainly fit the bill—a spinster, living all alone."

"Don't try to sell me that sob story. You're obviously a very sensible woman. And you're not as lonely as all that. You didn't have to invent a ghost to liven up your Saturday night now, did you? Your friends' cars were lining the curb all the way into the cul-de-sac."

"My secret's out—I'm a party girl," she said. "Actually the party was a little dull, so I thought I'd liven it up." Hysteria sharpened the edge of her attempted humor.

"With a ghost?" he said, calling the bluff on her flippancy. "If that were the case, you'd have come screaming into the house and told everyone all about it. But you didn't do that."

"Maybe I should have. Father Joe wouldn't have been able to deny it in front of everyone when he was so shaken."

Taylor lifted a stray wisp of hair from her forehead and tucked it behind her ear. "He was shaken?"

"More than I was. For me it was just the shock and the overwhelming feeling that the . . . that *whatever it was* was asking for help and I didn't know what to do. Father Joe must have felt his faith was being tested."

"You didn't get any sense of evil at all from it?"

She shook her head. "I couldn't stop thinking about it last night. I kept wondering who he was and why he appeared in that tree at that particular moment. I couldn't shake the feeling that whoever—or whatever—it was was asking for help, and I thought maybe he—*it*—had chosen that moment because it sensed a receptivity to compassion."

"You mean it was attracted to friendly vibrations in the house?"

"Yes. We'd had the house blessing ceremony. We were talking, laughing, enjoying ourselves. There was an atmosphere of . . . benevolence."

"And you think this *ghost*, for lack of any better word, tuned in to that with some sort of cosmic ESP?"

"I thought that in the middle of the night," she said. "I don't know what to think now, but I do know that I didn't get a sense of evil from this spirit, only desperation. I didn't feel threatened by it. And as repulsively ugly as it was, I wasn't afraid. I was concerned. I felt *compelled* to help it."

A tremor passed through her, and her voice was taut and high with the strain of fighting hysteria. "Maybe it *was* evil. Maybe it was luring me, preying on my better instincts, using them against me to hypnotize me. Or maybe it was totally unaware of me. Maybe it was just a random manifestation."

A burst of laughter revealed how close she was to losing the battle for control. "Maybe that same ghost goes from tree to tree all over the world. Maybe he has a regular routine. Maybe he hangs around my tree on alternate Saturday nights and then channels over to haunt some belfry during the week."

"Come here," Taylor said, drawing her to him by gently guiding her shoulders.

She went willingly and slid her arms around his waist and nestled her cheek against his chest. He was warm and solid—so humanly solid—and he smelled of soap and men's cologne. She clung to him, listening to the steady beating of that human heart, while he rocked her in his arms. A sigh of relief shuddered through her. How desperately she'd needed the touch, the comfort of another human being.

Several minutes passed in silence. Then Taylor said, "Do you want more wine?"

Vanessa raised her head from his chest. "No. I don't need it." She smiled. "I think I needed a hug more than anything else in the world."

"How would you feel about a kiss?"

She pretended to ponder the idea. "Do you kiss as good as you hug?"

"Better," he said, grinning cockily, and then proved it.

"I don't want to move," she said minutes later, after the kiss had evolved into a cozy embrace.

"I was considering seducing you before you sprang that ghost on me," he said. "The way you're snuggling up to me is giving the idea new life."

She pulled away from him reluctantly. "You can't seduce a woman with a ghost in her tree."

"Is that a hard-and-fast rule?"

"I don't know—this is my first ghost."

Taylor slapped his hands to his knees, indicating a readiness for action. "Let's bust the sucker!"

Vanessa frowned at him. "I don't know where to begin. Are we supposed to call in a sensitive? An exorcist?"

Taylor rose. "I think you should start by writing it down."

The wine on top of a sleepless night had dulled Vanessa's mind. "Writing what down?"

"Everything. Every detail—what it looked like, how big it was, what time you saw it, how long it was there, what you felt when you saw it."

"But why?"

"You should get it down on paper while it's still fresh in your mind. That way you'll have an accurate account if . . ." His voice trailed off, leaving the sentence dangling ominously.

"You think I'll see it again, don't you?" Vanessa asked somberly.

"I don't know." He brought his fisted hand to his lips and blew a gust of air through it in a gesture that mirrored her own frustration. "Who can say?"

"Who, indeed?" Vanessa murmured under her breath as she pulled herself off the lush cushions of the sofa. She took a legal tablet from a drawer in the kitchen and carried it to the small dining table in the breakfast nook.

She was still doodling artistic curlicues in the top margin when Taylor settled into the chair opposite hers.

"Do I have to put a full heading on this?" she asked, affecting the indolent attitude of her students.

"How do you stand being around wiseacre kids all day?" he asked.

"They're not so bad," Vanessa said. "You just have to ignore the typical teenage nonsense and try to deal with the real person inside. Underneath all that adolescent angst and arrogance, most of them are just scared kids trying to grow up."

"I was a hellion at that age. I don't know how my mother put up with me, much less how my teachers did."

"Usually hellions are angry about something," Vanessa said.

Taylor considered that a moment before admitting, "I *was* angry. About *everything*. Mostly, though, about my parents getting a divorce."

"And when you got in enough trouble, your mom had to call your dad?"

"Yes," he said with a chuckle of surprise. "I never realized that until now."

Vanessa smiled smugly. "Oh, you realized it. You just never acknowledged it."

He leveled a stare on her face. "It would have been interesting having you for a teacher. You're one formidable lady, you know that?"

Vanessa's smile faded. "To teenagers, maybe. To ghosts..."

"You are not going to let this defeat you," he said, his eyes still locked with hers. "Now write!"

"Yes, sir," Vanessa said, picking up her pen again. After a brief pause, she said, "Do you mind telling me what I'm supposed to be writing? I don't know how to begin."

"Last night at approximately—what time was it?"

"Ten-fifteen," Vanessa supplied as she wrote down what he dictated. She finished the phrase and cocked an eyebrow at him. "Pray, continue."

"Father Joe What's-his-name and I were standing approximately—how far away from the tree *were* you? How many feet?"

Panic edged her voice. "How am I supposed to know how many feet it was? Look, Taylor—"

"Write!" he said. "Leave blanks where you have to, and we'll take a tape out later and measure it."

"Bully!" she complained, resuming her writing. But, in fact, she was perfectly content with his bullying, which was quite benign. It felt better to be doing something than to be doing nothing; less futile to be taking some action, however futile the action itself; more productive to be doing something instead of brooding over not knowing what to do.

A quarter of an hour later, the account of what she'd seen was complete except for the blanks involving sizes and distances. Taylor took one look at the sixty-inch ribbon tape measure from Vanessa's sewing kit, rolled his eyes in exasperation and shook his head with the attitude of a man sorely put upon by life, then jogged to his house to get the industrial-size metal retracting measure from his tool kit.

He set about examining the tree and measuring what he considered to be relevant distances with crisp efficiency. Vanessa recorded the figures he called out—the exact length of the tree limb and the distance of the limb from the ground at highest and lowest points.

"Don't you think we could round off the nearest inch?" she asked when he called out a length that ended in seven-sixteenths.

He flashed her a sheepish grin as he rewound the tape. "I *was* rounding off. It's my carpentry background. I measure in thirty-seconds. Now, I want you to stand in the exact spot where you were when you first spied the figure in the tree."

"I'm not sure I can find the exact spot to the nearest thirty-second of an inch."

"Philistine," he said. "Just try for the closest inch."

"Closest foot is more like it," she grumbled, then fell silent while she tried to remember where she'd been the night before.

"Here," she said. "I was around this general area."

"Let's see," he said, taking the notebook out of her hands and poising the pen over the paper. "The house faces north . . ."

"I'm beginning to understand why you're so success-ful," Vanessa said.

"Which would make the tree east-southeast . . ."

"It's your ability to focus."

He shot evaluative glances at the two slopes of roof that met at the L of the house's structure, then began writing furiously in the notebook.

"I could take off my clothes right now, and you wouldn't even notice."

He raised his head to grin lasciviously. "Care to test me on that one?"

"What *are* you doing?"

"I'm orienting you, the house and the tree limb."

"Silly me for asking such a ridiculous question."

"Where was Father Joe? Direct me so I can stand where he was standing."

"We had just put the bag in the trash can, so he was walking right behind me."

Taylor traced the route she'd described. "How far was he from you when he stopped?"

"I don't know."

"Try to remember."

"I couldn't possibly remember because I was looking at the figure in the tree. And quit being such a tyrant!"

"Does wine make you irritable, or are you naturally grumpy?"

"I just don't like being ordered around."

"I'm sorry if I seem bossy. I guess I've gotten too used to giving orders at work." He cupped her chin in his hand and tilted her face toward his. "My intentions are pure, even if my method is clumsy. I'm trying to help you."

She breathed out a sigh. "I know. And I appreciate it. But I don't see what good orienting me on paper is going to do."

"Think about it, Vanessa. Either what you saw was a ghost, or it was something else. If it was something else, then it must have been a projected image of some sort. A hologram, most likely."

"Someone's idea of fun? But who . . . and how? And how would anyone know we were going to be outside at that moment?"

"That's just the point. They wouldn't have to. Someone could have been out riding around until they spied a party. They could have set it up just gambling that someone would come outside at some point. That's why where you were might have been crucial to what you saw. If it was a hologram, then what you saw might be an indicator of where the projector might have been."

"How common are hologramic projectors?"

"Not very. I'd be willing to bet they cost a pretty penny."

"So it would have to be someone sadistic but affluent."

"They wouldn't necessarily have to own the equipment. They might just have access to it."

A thoughtful silence followed before Taylor said, "You're frowning. What are you thinking?"

"Something I don't want to think, much less believe."

"Which is?"

"After I heard the screams, Karen Lake—a friend of mine—suggested that one of my students might have been playing a prank on me."

Before he could jump on the idea, which his face clearly showed he was about to do, she said adamantly, "It's just not feasible, Taylor. I doubt there's a hologramic projector in the county, much less one that any of my students could get their hands on. And even if it was possible, it wouldn't explain . . ." The sentence died prematurely in a weary sigh.

"What?" he prompted.

"The way I felt," she said softly.

An ominous silence hung in the air between them for what seemed like a very long time. He didn't believe her about the ghost any more than anyone had believed her about the screams. She was so sure about both, yet didn't they say that when you thought you were the only sane person and everyone else was crazy, it was a good sign you were the crazy one?

"Think about it, Vanessa. It was pitiful and you wanted to help it. Don't you see that that reaction came from within you, not necessarily from the figure? You responded to it the way you would respond to a lost, hungry puppy."

"But it wasn't like that. It wasn't a normal feeling of pity. It was more like a compulsion. Yes, a compulsion," she repeated, savoring the correctness of the word.

"You were shaken when you saw it. It's only natural that your reactions would seem intense after an emotional shock."

"You don't understand," she said. "I can't explain it, but I was being summoned to help."

"A perfectly normal urge might seem like a compulsion under the circumstances."

"Didn't you have something else you wanted to measure?" Vanessa said sharply. "To the nearest thirty-second of an inch?"

Taylor dipped to kiss the tip of her nose and gave her the end of the metal tape. "Hold on to this, Miss Wiggins."

He walked to the tree and stood under the limb. "Where was the figure hanging?"

"To your left a couple of feet—and thirteen thirty-seconds."

"Here?" he asked, ignoring her gibe.

"Another inch or two. Yes, there."

Taylor read the tape, made a notation in the notebook. "You can let go now," he said.

Vanessa dropped the tape and it whizzed across the lawn as Taylor pressed the retractor button on the case. Suspending it on the belt loop of his pants, he tossed the notebook down on the grass and, with a single fluid motion, leaped up to hook his hands over the limb. Then, with a few calculated swings of his body, he hooked his right leg over the limb. From that point, it was a simple matter to settle himself astride it.

Vanessa forgot her pique as she admired the lithe grace in his economical movements, the evident strength of his body.

"What are you doing now?" she asked.

"Looking for anything unusual."

In addition to his strength, she envied him his non-chalance—the nonchalance that came from not having seen a ghost he was certain didn't exist, the smug nonchalance that grew out of humoring someone when deep down you knew they were wrong and you were right. Anger seeped in to undermine her gratitude for his comfort, his companionship, his very presence when she'd needed the touch of someone human and alive. "Finding anything?"

Taylor swiped at his left forearm with the fingers of his right hand. "An occasional ant." Meticulously studying each inch of bark as he moved, he eased his way to the trunk of the tree, stood and shimmied up to a higher limb, which he examined just as meticulously. Every juncture, every limb fell under his scrutiny.

"You're going to break your neck," Vanessa called as she watched his reckless descent after he'd examined even the uppermost branches.

"An old tree climber like me? No way," he said without pausing in his downward spiral. He reached the lowest limb and dropped to the ground. His sneakers produced a dull thud as they landed on the packed earth beneath the tree. "My mother always accused me of being part monkey." He flashed her a grin as he brushed flecks of bark and dust from his clothes. "And then I'd counter by accusing her of monkeying around with Tarzan."

The grin faded as he moved close enough to put his hand on her shoulder and gave it a reassuring squeeze. "I didn't find anything out of the ordinary."

"I don't even know what you were looking for."

"Rope fibers, scars in the bark, nail holes. Signs that someone had been climbing in there, that something had been mounted on one of the limbs—"

"A projector?" she challenged hostilely.

"I don't know, damn it! And neither do you, so quit blaming me for all the unanswered questions."

She buried her face in her hands. "I didn't mean to do that. I'm sorry."

He pulled her hands to his lips and kissed them. "I'm sorry I snapped at you. It's just . . . it's a damned frustrating situation."

"You don't have to get involved," she said. "It's not really your problem, you know."

"Isn't it? Wolf Corner is my baby. Do you think I want word getting around that it's haunted?"

She bristled. "I can see where that might hurt sales."

Taylor dropped her hands. "Do you think that's why I'm here?"

*It's why you just happened to jog past after the cops told you about the screams*, she thought. But there was no way he could have known about the ghost. "I don't know what to think," she admitted. Her eyes met his in challenge. "Why are you here?"

"Because I have a neighbor I'm concerned about." That slow, easy grin slid into place. "And because you have a great behind."

*Cropville, Texas—1945*

INA TWIGG hesitantly poked her head into Jessica's office. "I hate to bother you, but there's a Mr. Bannerson in the lobby. He doesn't have an account, and he doesn't want a loan application, but he insists—"

"Mr. Bannerson, you say?" Jessica asked incredulously. Two months had passed since the victory celebration, and Jessica had repeatedly dismissed Danny Bannerson from her thoughts, categorizing him as a blurry-faced pen pal forever in her past.

"That's right. Bannerson. Must not be from around here. I've never seen him before." Ina stood in the doorway, obviously hoping for an explanation from Jessica about the mystery man in the lobby.

Ina's curiosity was not to be appeased. Jessica closed the file she'd been reading, drummed her fingertips on the desktop as she thought over the situation, then said, "Wait about five minutes and then send him in."

Disappointment made Ina's face droop, but she nodded, then left.

Jessica was not a person prone to panic, but a wave of that alien emotion swept over her as she fumbled in her desk drawer for a mirror and applied fresh lipstick with an unsteady hand. She smoothed her hair and adjusted the scarf tied around the bun perched at the nape of her neck, then brushed the lapels of her suit jacket.

Hat in hand, Bannerson entered her office as tentatively as someone approaching a bomb that could explode at any moment and nodded a self-conscious greeting. He was of moderate height and solidly built. His dark brown hair was still in a military cut. Jessica couldn't distinguish the color of his eyes from across the office, but she was aware of their intensity as he scrutinized her unabashedly.

Forcing herself not to fidget, she met his gaze head-on. Finally he laughed, and the pleasant sound of his laughter shattered the awkward tension of the moment. "You look like a bank president," he said, smiling. "You're wearing a gray flannel suit."

"And you," she said lightly, "look like an ex-marine. Hank Bruner's blue-ribbon bull couldn't knock you down."

"Hello, Jessica," he said.

"Hello, Danny," she replied. "Welcome to Cropville."

# 5

VANESSA STOOD behind the front door as she opened it, stretching her neck just far enough to see who was there. "Taylor?"

"I've figured it out," he said. Without waiting for a formal invitation, he brushed past the door into the living room.

"You're fully dressed," Vanessa said.

"I've got to be on-site by seven. I figured you'd be up, too."

"You were not quite half-right."

"Do you have coffee?"

"In a bag in the cupboard," Vanessa said.

"Don't make it unless you usually do. I can wait until I get to work."

"It's six o'clock in the morning, Taylor," Vanessa said. "I'm not dressed."

Taylor gave her an evaluative once-over, from her tousled hair to her silky jacquard robe to her pink-polished toenails, and then dropped a kiss on her cheek. "You look good in the morning, sweetheart, but are you always this grouchy?"

"Only when certain people camp out in my living room all Sunday evening lulling me with wine and pizza and keep me up past midnight watching old movies, then wrest me out of deep sleep by sitting on the doorbell before my alarm clock gets to the second snooze."

"I'll make coffee if you point me in the right direction. It might sweeten up your disposition. Now go get some clothes on before I jump your bones."

"You're almost as bossy in the morning as you are the rest of the time," Vanessa countered. "Coffee's in the cupboard to the right of the sink, pot's in the cabinet directly below. You're on your own for earplugs."

"Earplugs?"

She flashed him a saccharine smile over her shoulder as she entered the hallway to the back of the house. "I'm going to take a shower and I might sing."

By the time she returned, scrubbed and dressed and with her hair curling damply around her face, he was seated at the breakfast nook table nursing a mug of steaming coffee. She went directly into the kitchen to pour herself a cup. "I can't face teenagers without breakfast," she said. "Would you like a bowl of cereal?"

"As long as it doesn't have marshmallows or stars in it."

"Now," she said, after serving them both and taking a seat opposite him, "what's important enough for six o'clock in the morning?"

"Your ghost, of course," he said. "Hey, this isn't bad. I suppose it's nourishing."

"High fiber."

"I figured as much."

"What about my ghost?"

"I got to thinking last night."

"After you went home? It was past midnight."

"I don't sleep well when I'm sexually frustrated."

Vanessa harrumphed skeptically. "You don't look as though your growth has been stunted by lack of sleep."

"If what you saw was a ghost, then it had to be the ghost of someone."

"Now why didn't I think of that?"

"For a teacher, you have a pretty fresh mouth."

"It's the coffee. I was comatose, but now I'm wide-awake and furious."

"Listen, would you? If this is the ghost of someone who actually lived, then it may be linked to this area for some reason. And if so, then someone else may have seen it."

"You mean before Saturday night."

"It could be hundreds of years old."

"And it could come back at any moment," Vanessa said. "That's *not* a cheering thought."

"Look, lady, I've never believed in ghosts, but I've seen my share of haunted house movies, and there's always a reason ghosts are roaming around, something that's left unsettled at the time of death."

"Another reassuring thought this early in the morning. I've not only got a ghost, I've got one bent on revenge."

"You said he wanted help of some kind."

Vanessa shivered. "Let's hope he's decided I'm not the one he needs."

"You really are in a weird mood this morning," Taylor commented.

"I did a little thinking myself last night—very little, I'll admit, but enough to realize that I'd be much better off if the uninvited guest at my party was a hologram. Today I'm going to do a little research into how difficult it would be for certain of my students to get their hands on a hologramic projector."

"You've changed your mind about what you saw? Yesterday you were pretty adamant about what you felt."

She shrugged. "Like you said, I probably just reacted to the sight the way I would react to anything in trouble."

"You're not fooling me, lady, and I don't think you're fooling yourself."

"What are you, intent on playing the devil's advocate? Yesterday you were sure—"

"I wasn't sure of anything. I had an opinion. You were the one who was sure. Now you're doubting yourself."

Vanessa put down her spoon and looked him squarely in the face. Her eyes were large and full of silent pleading. Taylor thought he would see terror there if he delved deep enough into their depths. "I've got a woman screaming outside my window and a man in a late stage of decomposition hanging in my tree. Either my house is haunted or some student is playing tricks on me. Which alternative would you choose?"

"The truth," Taylor said softly. "And I think you would, too. That's why I'm going to help you find it. While you're checking out the hologramic projectors, I'm going to find out who owned this property before the money-grubbing investment firm I bought it from."

Vanessa studied the granola swimming in her bowl with undue interest. So much for convincing herself she hadn't seen what she saw; she couldn't even convince a near stranger that she believed it was anything other than a ghost.

The antique clock on the mantel chimed the half hour, and Taylor glanced at his watch as though he couldn't believe so much time had passed. He took one final spoonful of cereal and drained the orange juice

Vanessa had set before him, then rose, picking up his dishes to carry them to the kitchen. "Thanks for the breakfast, beautiful, but I've got to get on-site. I'll talk to you tonight."

"Taylor," she called after him tentatively.

He poked his head around the corner and cocked an eyebrow inquiringly.

"Why?" she said, and they both knew what she was asking.

He gave her a cunning grin. "Aside from the fact that I'm basically a nice guy, I can't seduce you as long as you have that ghost in your tree."

"VANESSA. HELLO."

Vanessa gasped and leaped an inch from the chair behind the desk.

"Sorry," Laura Gaines said. "I didn't mean to startle you."

"I didn't hear you come in."

"Obviously. You were in a trance. What's up?"

Vanessa's left hand was resting atop the file of personal information cards, and the fingers of her right hand were fanned over the list of names she'd brought into the guidance office. "I'm just checking on a few students' home situations, parents' occupations."

Laura reached for the list. "May I?"

"Oh.... Sure," Vanessa said, wondering what she would tell Laura if pressed for an explanation of how and why she had compiled the assortment of names. It was harrowing enough going through class rosters trying to pinpoint students who might get a real thrill out of scaring their teacher out of her wits, without having to explain to the eleventh-grade counselor that either her students were playing cruel tricks on her or her new house was haunted.

"An eclectic group," Laura commented, putting the list back on the desk without pressing for details. "Are you finding what you need?" When Vanessa nodded, Laura said, "I'll leave it to you, then. I've got parents due any second, and I like to be in my office looking busy when they arrive. If you hit any dead ends or need anything I can help you with, feel free to ask."

Vanessa's smile was genuine. Laura was a fine counselor—good at reading people, anxious to help them, careful not to crowd them. "Thanks, Laura. I'll remember you said that."

In less than ten minutes she was finished with her search, and what she'd found was less than promising. The parents of students in this high school were a microcosm of suburban American life: a supermarket manager, a secretary, two oil field workers, a plumber, an insurance salesman, a mechanic, an attorney, a nurse, a florist. No photographers or anyone connected with photography. Her only lead was Heather McQueen's mother, who had described her job as advertising account representative.

Vanessa's hands were almost shaking as she punched in the phone number of the agency. Her throat was cotton dry as she counted the rings before a crisp voice came over the line with, "Good afternoon. Franklin Ad Agency."

"I was interested . . ." Vanessa swallowed and started over. "I had an idea for a special event that calls for a holographic projector, and I was wondering if your agency—"

"We don't do anything like that," the woman said. "We're a small agency specializing in novelty promotional items like pens, buttons, hats and balloons."

Vanessa exhaled raggedly, moving the mouthpiece of the phone away so that the woman on the line wouldn't hear.

"I'm sorry," the woman said into the sudden silence.

"Do you . . . do you know where I might find a hologramic projector? Another agency, perhaps?"

"I don't, I'm sorry," the woman told her. "Maybe one of the major ad agencies could direct you somewhere."

"I'm starting from scratch on this," Vanessa said. "Can you recommend one?"

"I can't recommend one, but I can give you the names of a couple of the larger agencies."

Vanessa wrote down the names of the agencies and thanked the receptionist. There wasn't enough time to call the agencies before her last two classes, so she looked up the numbers in the telephone directory and tucked the list of names and numbers in her purse. She'd make the calls from her house after school, where there was less chance of being overheard or interrupted.

The wisteria and roses had turned cloying with age. The combined scents of the aging blossoms assaulted Vanessa's nostrils as she entered the house. She headed straight for the back windows to open them, sneezing once on the way, glad it was a mild spring and that the heat and humidity had not yet forced her to turn on the air conditioning.

Eventually Vanessa hoped to get ceiling fans for the main rooms of the house, but for now she had to rely on a box fan she'd placed on the floor near the windows. Satisfied that the stale air in the living room was beginning to stir, she went to her bedroom to put on jeans and a soft chambray shirt, then padded back to the front of the house, barefoot, to pour herself a glass of juice. She carried it to the telephone, where her answering machine indicated there had been an incoming call, but no message had been left on the tape. Some kind of phone solicitor, no doubt; her family and friends knew her work schedule.

She rewound the tape and reset the machine, then picked up her purse before settling into the armchair next to the phone table to call the first advertising agency on her list. She was referred to an account executive, who, in turn, referred her to an audio visual specialty firm.

What she learned both chilled and reassured her. She'd *known* that what she'd seen hadn't been a projected beam of light, but this was one time when she'd have preferred to find out she'd been mistaken. Unfortunately, all the evidence pointed to the conclusion that she'd been right about what she'd seen.

Restless suddenly, she gathered a load of towels and threw them into the washer, hand washed her lingerie, then moved outside to work off her excess energy on the flower bed she was putting in to accommodate the wisteria cuttings Margaret had brought her.

When the waning sun forced her to give up on her gardening, Vanessa went inside to shower. Ordinarily she would have put on a knit sleep shirt to lounge around in, but tonight, on a whim, she wandered around the walk-in closet in search of something more elegant. She settled on a lavender gauze caftan that fell to her ankles in soft folds from an elasticized peasant neckline.

Standing in front of the wall mirror, she shoved the elastic off her shoulders, baring them. Her hair, still

damp, was cool against the skin on her back. She felt
feminine, pretty, pleased with the way she looked as she
primped, striking coquettish poses at her reflection.
Taylor would . . .

The truth of it hit her suddenly: she was waiting on
Taylor. She was growing accustomed to his im-
promptu visits and dependent on his calm, analytical
viewpoint. He had been there, ready to listen and console when she'd needed a willing ear and someone to
lean on, and she had been pouring out her problems
and drawing on his strength. He had become her friend,
her ally, her sounding board.

Because she had let him.

Now, as she wore a frilly caftan and stood monkey-
shining in front of the mirror like an adolescent
schoolgirl hoping he'd drop by, she realized she was in
danger of letting him become more. She adjusted the
gathers of the peasant neckline, fluffed her hair with a
toss of her head and blew a flirtatious kiss at her re-
flected image. *Qué será, será!*

Conscious now that she was waiting for Taylor, Vanessa grew even more restless. She returned to the living room to get started on the research papers she hoped
to finish grading by the end of the week, but as she
stepped from the hallway the blended scents of wisteria and roses drew her attention to the vases on the
end table. She'd put them there hoping the draft might
keep them fresh. It had worked for the roses; with a
change of water they would last another day or two.
The wisteria, however, never a hardy flower for cutting, was irredeemably beyond its prime.

Deciding she might as well take it to the kitchen and
empty it into the plastic-lined garbage pail, Vanessa
picked up the vase of wisteria. Petals rained from the

stems at the movement. Thinking she would have to bring the mountain—in this case, the trash pail—to Mohammed, Vanessa went to the kitchen for it.

Outside, a cold front was moving in rapidly from the northwest. Riding the edge of that front, the wind had cooled and intensified. Abrupt gusts whipped through the limbs of the oak tree, rustling the young spring leaves, and then shoved through the window screens. Just as Vanessa lifted the vase again, a strong current of chill air captured the aged wisteria, tearing the limp petals free from the stems and lifting them up and away. Time seemed as suspended as the petals as the purple, tissue-light discs hung in the current of wind. A shiver tingled along Vanessa's spine as she watched the aerial ballet and the cold air strained through the open weave of the gauze caftan.

For a few brief seconds the petals spun and twirled in unison, almost as though they might reunite in some new, definitive shape. Then, as the wind lost its momentum and surrendered the fragile petals to gravity's influence, Vanessa stepped to the windows and slammed them closed, shutting out the cold wind. She yielded to an involuntary shudder of cold, then switched off the box fan and began picking up the scattered petals. They were everywhere—on the end table, the arm of the sofa, the carpet—and they had to be picked up individually. Any attempt to gather or scoop them into a stack only curled them into moist, uncooperative little balls that left sap stains.

"Texas!" Vanessa grumbled as she got down on her hands and knees to clean the petals off the carpet one by one. "If you don't like the weather, wait five minutes and it'll change. The only state in the Union where you have to study the weather forecasts before you open a window!"

Another chill slid up her spine as a fresh current of air wafted through the caftan and ruffled the petals on the floor. Allowing a momentary truce in the Battle of the Fallen Wisteria, she sat back on her haunches, hugging herself against the cold, and shot a glare of impotent disgust at the windows she'd closed and locked. The draft in this corner wasn't a figment of anyone's imagination. Customer service was going to get a call tomorrow.

At length she finished cleaning up the floral debris and decided to raid the cold cuts left over from the party for dinner. She carried her plate to the living room and settled on the sofa with her papers and a red pen to read the varying accounts of how federal laws are made. Most of her students had a general grasp of the process. The more meticulous ones gave her detailed accounts gleaned directly from the textbook and received A minuses; the less precise summarized the general steps and were awarded B pluses; a small percentage invented whole new processes that had nothing to do with reality. Vanessa posted a D plus on a paper from the latter group, thinking it would have earned an A for creativity in a writing class.

The clock on the mantel chimed nine times, and a niggling disappointment swelled in her chest. The chances of Taylor Stephenson paying one of his surprise visits were dwindling with each swing of the pendulum. She put her papers aside, stretched her arms in the air, sucked in a deep breath and tried to remember how long it had been since she'd sat around waiting on a man to call or drop in. With a sniff of self-disgust, she picked up the next paper to read about bills and committees.

Under siege of the abruptly dropping temperature outside, the house had cooled gradually. Vanessa paused in her reading long enough to pull down the afghan that had been draped over the back of the couch and tuck it around her legs. She nudged her shoulders deeper into the stack of throw pillows.

The lawmaking process had never seem so monotonous....

*Escape. Have to escape. Light. The window. Running toward it. Have to get away. Clock ticking. Louder. Louder. Crawling. Unable to walk. Leg hurting. Clock ticking, ticking. Bong! Bong!*

Vanessa jerked awake, springing into a sitting position. The sheer terror of the dream lingered. Her breath was coming in gulps; her heart was pounding. The dream clock was still bonging, but it was no longer a bong, it was a ring. The telephone.

She groped for the receiver, knocked it off the cradle, retrieved it. "Hello?" She said it while inhaling instead of exhaling, so it came out as an uncertain squeal.

"Vanessa? What's wrong?"

"Taylor?"

"Is something wrong?"

"I dozed off while I was grading papers. I . . . I was dreaming," she said vaguely. "There was a window. And a clock."

Her voice was still thick with sleep. An image of the way she'd looked when she'd answered the door that morning—heavy lidded, bed rumpled, sexy as hell—established itself in Taylor's mind.

"That doesn't sound like a very sexy dream," he observed.

"Something was chasing me."

"I hope it was me."

"It was a nightmare," she said.

"Then it couldn't have been me."

Vanessa's head was clearing. The dream was not difficult to analyze. The window she'd closed earlier, the clock she'd checked just before she fell asleep—the clock ticking away her hope that Taylor would drop by, her apprehension that he wouldn't. She wasn't about to offer up any of her analysis to Taylor's ego.

After a silence, Taylor said, "Are you okay?"

"My students are off the hook," Vanessa said gravely.

"What did you find out?"

"There's no such thing as a hologramic projector— at least not anything as simple as a single piece of machinery someone could point at a spot and produce a realistic ghost. There's a process that creates the illusion of a three-dimensional image, but it's very complicated, involving beam splitters and specially coated glass surfaces."

"Is this beam splitter anything your students could build or get access to?"

"It's too high tech. Strictly Hollywood stuff and then only used by a handful of experienced technicians. It's not something that could be done without advance preparation or telltale signs."

"So we're back to the original theory."

"A ghost, you mean? It's not a theory anymore, as far as I'm concerned."

"You never bought the practical joke theory in the first place, did you?"

"I was only trying to fool myself into thinking I believed it."

"Look, if you need company, I can—"

"That's not necessary. It's not as though he's come back for another visit."

"Are you sure you're all right, you're handling it okay?"

"Now that you've got me wide-awake, I'm going to watch the evening news and finish grading my papers."

Another pause. "For what it's worth, I did a little digging myself. The agent who handled the Wolf Corner purchase for me is going to find out about previous owners. Maybe we can learn if your transparent little friend has a history of showing up uninvited. If we can discover whose ghost it is, maybe . . ."

She'd seen a ghost. There was no other explanation. All afternoon she'd held the full realization of it at bay, but now that she was talking about it, the shock was sinking in and hysteria was threatening to close in on her.

"Maybe I can greet it by name next time he materializes?" she asked. "Maybe strike up a conversation? 'Hello, Mr. Ghost, how are things going in the spirit world? Hung from any interesting trees lately?'"

Taylor picked up the note of hysteria in her voice. "I'm coming over."

"That's not necessary."

"It is for me."

"Taylor, it's late. . . ."

"I'll be there by the time the news is over. Don't be alarmed when you hear the doorbell."

Good as his word, he arrived just as the end titles on the news flashed onto the screen. He was carrying a brown shopping bag, which he took straight to the kitchen and deposited on the counter.

Vanessa followed. "Just make yourself right at home."

Ignoring her sarcasm, he said, "Don't worry about me. I will." And he did just that, moving around the kitchen as if he owned it, opening the cabinet where she kept her coffee. "I believe I saw some decaf this morning. Ah, yes. Here it is."

"What are you doing?"

"Making Irish coffee," he said, unplugging the coffeepot so he could throw out the morning's grounds and rinse it. He filled the pot, spooned fresh grounds into the basket and plugged it back in.

"Irish coffee? With whiskey?"

"Uh-huh. Real whipped cream, too. Luckily the convenience store next to the liquor store had some. Get some mugs down and I'll show you how to coat the rims with sugar."

"I *know* how to dip mugs in sugar," she said.

"Great! That leaves me free to whip the cream, if you'll get me a bowl and a whip."

The nerve of the man, dropping in at the crack of dawn or the middle of night, taking over her kitchen, ordering her around like his personal sous-chef. "I'll get you a whip, all right," she mumbled under her breath.

Unfortunately, he heard her. "You're not into kink, are you?" he teased, earning a scowl. "I was referring to the wire whips you use in the kitchen."

Vanessa opened the drawer where she kept her utensils, fished out a wire whip and slapped it into his hand. "The mixing bowls are in the cupboard to the left. Help yourself."

*Yes, ma'am*, Taylor thought, wondering what he'd done to raise her ire. He decided on a course of prudent silence over overt confrontation and turned his attention to whipping the cream.

"The mugs are ready," Vanessa said a couple of minutes later.

"The cream's almost there, too. Here, keep whipping while I open the whiskey." He shoved the bowl into her arms. "It's all in the wrist," he said lightly, demonstrating by drawing circles in the air. She was glowering at him as though he'd asked her to clean a parking lot with a toothbrush. Undaunted, he said, "You know, if you keep hugging the bowl that way, it's going to get warm and it'll take forever to get the cream to peak."

She set the bowl on the table and began whipping in circular motions with near violent fervor.

"Talk about timing," he said after measuring whiskey into the mugs, "the coffeepot just shut off. Cream ready?"

"I just need to stir in some sugar."

"Let's do it, then!" He dolloped cream atop the whiskey-laced coffee and sculptured it into a cloud with the back of the spoon before handing her the first cup. "Here you go. Just what the doctor ordered."

"You're not my doctor, Taylor."

"I'm not your adversary, either." He wrapped his fingers around her upper arm gently, demanding her attention.

She turned her face toward his. "Why are you here?"

Taylor dropped his hand, picked up his mug and stared at the patterns in the cloud of cream. "I'm beginning to ask myself the same question. I came because I was concerned. You sounded as if you could use some company and a stiff drink."

Vanessa walked to the sofa and sat down, carefully balancing the mug while she folded her legs under her and nudged the throw pillows with her shoulders until she had burrowed out a comfortable niche. Taylor sat next to her.

She swirled her forefinger through the cream on her coffee and then licked the residue off her finger. "You like being needed, don't you?"

"Everybody likes being needed."

Vanessa took a tentative sip of the drink, registering the grainy sweetness of the sugar, the smoothness of the cream, the steaming heat of the spiked coffee. A second sip burned her throat and broadcast a spreading warmth through her chest. She gave Taylor a small smile. "Especially by women?"

"The more beautiful the better," he said, grinning in a way that told her he was mocking her just a bit.

She took another sip of the coffee. The cream had softened enough to give it an interesting texture. "This *was* a good idea," she admitted grudgingly. "Although after wine yesterday and whiskey tonight, I may be chugalugging moonshine straight from the jug by the end of the week."

"Strictly medicinal," Taylor said.

"I'll remember that at my first AA meeting."

"You've had a shock. It'll relax you, help you sleep."

"If I do manage to fall asleep, do you promise not to wake me up again?"

"Are you really angry about this morning, or are you just venting rage at me because I'm handy?"

She frowned at him from behind her coffee mug, then took a long draft. The bite of the whiskey brought tears to her eyes. "It's not as much fun being a damsel in distress as it is being the compassionate hero."

He raised his right hand to cradle her face and stroked her cheek gently with his thumb. "Do you want to talk about it or talk about something else to get your mind off it?"

"I keep wondering why it—what's the word?—materialized, and if it'll come back."

"Maybe if we find out whose ghost it is, we'll also find out whether it's ever been seen before." He lowered his hand.

"I'm growing to hate that word."

"What word is that?" Taylor asked, his voice soothing.

"'Maybe,'" she said. She drained what remained of her coffee in a single gulp and then licked the residue of cream and sugar from her lips.

"I wish you'd let me do that," Taylor said, raising his hand again to trace her still moist lips with his thumb.

"Could you just hold me for a while, instead?"

"You asked why I'm here," Taylor said, taking Vanessa's mug from her hand and placing it alongside his own on the end table. He stretched his arm across the back of the sofa, inviting her to move next to him. "This is why."

# 6

"CAN'T FIND A THING WRONG."

Vanessa gave the man from customer service an exasperated frown. His name was Tom Burleigh, which was quite fitting, since burly described him aptly. He was a large man who, in tight jeans and cotton T-shirt, looked as though he might have just left one of the construction crews. For a quarter of an hour he'd been running his plump fingertips along window seams and floor molding and poking his hand under the bottom shingles of Vanessa's back wall.

"But you can *feel* the draft," she said, hugging her arms as if in emphasis.

Burleigh shrugged. "Houses have drafts sometimes. Who knows why? Could be the chimney updrafting."

"I keep the flue closed when I'm not using the fireplace," she said.

He shrugged again. "All I can tell you for sure is that it's nothing structural. The windows are tight and there's nothing wrong with the slab. You could try some foam insulation under the shingles. Sometimes that helps."

"How about the walls?" Vanessa asked.

"We always double-check the insulation before sealing the walls. We'd have found any tears or thin spots or kinks."

Vanessa frowned. For this she'd rushed home from work? So some clown from customer service could tell her her draft was a draft and so what? "You've certainly got an answer for everything," she said.

Burleigh didn't catch the irony in the statement. "Yes, ma'am," he agreed, extending his clipboard toward her. "We'll need your signature that I was here. Sign by the X."

Vanessa took the board and read the form. "This says that the necessary repairs have been ordered."

"Can't repair what isn't broken," Burleigh said, growing impatient.

"Is there a way I can acknowledge that you were here but that I'm not satisfied that nothing's been done?"

"There's a comment line," he replied grudgingly.

She made a notation and signed the form, then returned the clipboard. To her surprise, Burleigh was cupping a rose in his beefy palm. "Nice roses," he said. "Smelled them when I walked in." He took the clipboard. "My wife likes roses. I always send her some on our anniversary."

"That's very nice."

"Smell always reminds me of my grandmother's funeral."

*A true romantic!* Vanessa thought.

"Well, I got other calls to make," Burleigh said, starting for the door. He was reaching for the doorknob when the doorbell rang. He turned back to Vanessa. "Sounds like you got company."

She gestured for him to open the door.

"Mr. Stephenson!" he exclaimed, snapping to attention with all the consternation of a shavetail lieutenant who'd suddenly come face-to-face with a general.

Taylor, stepping into the entryway, seemed almost as surprised. "Burleigh? What's up?"

Burleigh seemed to have lost his faculty for speech, so it was Vanessa who said, "I called customer service about the draft. I thought perhaps one of the windows—"

"Find anything?" Taylor asked Burleigh.

"No, sir," Burleigh said. "I checked 'em all out thoroughly. The slab, too."

"Nothing?"

Burleigh shook his head somberly. "Not a thing." After a beat, he suggested, "Could be a weird updraft from the chimney."

Taylor looked at Vanessa. "We'll have to check that out."

"Well," Burleigh interjected abruptly, clearly uncomfortable in the presence of his boss. He gestured to his clipboard. "I've got a bunch of calls to make. Unless you want me to recheck—"

"That won't be necessary," Taylor said. "I'm sure you were as careful and thorough as always."

"Yes, sir," he said. "Well, goodbye."

"What do you do, discipline your employees with a cat-o'-nine-tails?" Vanessa asked drolly after Burleigh bolted through the door.

"Some people are intimidated by authority," Taylor said. "He doesn't have any reason to fear me if he's doing his job." He drew Vanessa into his arms and then cupped her chin in his right palm, tilting her face toward his. "Tell me, as a customer, what was your opinion? Was he doing his job, or should he be sweating?"

"He did the best he could."

"Your enthusiasm wouldn't get a helium-filled balloon off the ground. Problem?"

"I just wish he'd found something fixable. That draft is very pronounced. My utility bills are going to be astronomical if air gets out the way it gets in."

"I'm going to have to check out your chimney," he said, but the words themselves held less meaning than the sensuous timbre of his voice and the subtle movement of his arm, which anchored her body more snugly against his. "Can't afford to have a dissatisfied home owner." His mouth hovered so close to hers that the murmured words teased over her lips in a preamble of the kiss that was imminent.

It was the first time he'd kissed her when she wasn't overwrought and preoccupied, the first time she'd been at emotional liberty to wholly enjoy his touching her the way a woman enjoyed being touched by a man. Always before she had clung to him as a fellow human being, as a source of reassurance as well as a source of pleasure.

Taylor must have sensed the lowering of her defenses, the abandonment with which she surrendered herself to the sensual delights of the kiss, because when the kiss had ended, he grinned down at her and said, "You sure kiss good when you're not thinking about ghosts."

Vanessa gave him a playful jab in the ribs and laughed. "You ought to try me when I'm really in the mood."

"I plan to," Taylor said, "but you'll just have to contain your more libidinous urges for the present. We've got a woman to see about a ghost."

Taylor had phoned the school that morning and left an urgent message for Vanessa to call him at his office. When she returned the call during her conference period, he'd said, "I've found a woman we ought to talk

to, a real estate agent named Phelps. She says she can
see us tonight if we can get to Alief by six-fifteen. Can
you make it?"

"Sure, but—"

"Look, Vanessa, I'm sorry, but I'm in the middle of a
minor crisis here. I'll pick you up at your house a little
after five, okay?" He'd barely waited for her acquiescent "Okay" before hanging up.

Vanessa had spent the rest of her conference period
at the library. Now she picked up the book she'd
checked out on the way out to Taylor's car. "Tell me
about this woman we're going to see," she said as Taylor drove toward the neighboring suburbs of Alief.
"Think she'll be able to tell us anything?"

"She's one of the best leads we've got," Taylor said.
"Her father bought the land back in 1946 and owned it
until he died in the late sixties. She inherited it and sold
it to the investment corporation—for a tidy little profit,
no doubt—when land started escalating and taxes es-
calated along with it."

"You say she's a real estate agent?"

"Yes. Apparently a very successful one. I've heard of
her company."

"Does she know why we're coming?"

"Not specifically. I fudged and just told her we
wanted to talk about some land. She might have put me
off if I'd gone into detail on the phone, but she can
hardly kick us out when we've driven a distance to talk
to her. Besides," he added, chancing a glance away from
the traffic to raise his eyebrows at her mischievously,
"this way, I get to take you to dinner."

Vanessa thumbed through the slender book she'd
brought along. "I checked this out of the school library. It was the only book they had on ghosts and

ghostlore. It doesn't look very comprehensive, but maybe it'll cover the basics."

"Finding out anything interesting?" Taylor asked a few minutes later. Engrossed in the book, Vanessa had become very quiet.

"The first few pages were pretty general," she said. "You know, no one knows whether or not ghosts actually exist, but there have been reports of ghosts and hauntings throughout recorded history. There seem to be three schools of thought—that ghosts exist, that ghosts do not exist and that ghosts *could* exist."

"Not exactly Pulitzer-caliber reporting, is it?"

"The second chapter looks promising—'Fundamentals of Ghostlore.' Listen. 'While no evidence has ever proven the existence of ghosts, it is generally believed that ghosts that reveal themselves to people in a humanlike form are spiritual manifestations of human beings who once actually lived.'"

"Sherlock!"

Still absorbed in the book, Vanessa reported, "Apparently poltergeists—'noisy ghosts,' literally translated—are something different." She read a few more paragraphs silently, then chuckled and turned to Taylor. "They seem to be the practical jokers of the spirit world, playing juvenile pranks."

"A far cry from the demons from hell in the teen thrillers, huh?"

"Yes, although they seem to have a particular interest in prepubescent children and . . ."

"What?"

"Men of the cloth," she completed.

"Father Joe."

"It's apples and oranges, Taylor. If my tree is haunted, it's by a legitimate ghost, not some cosmic prankster."

Taylor refrained from commenting.

"The image I saw was distinctly human derivative, and it says here poltergeists make no effort to assume human form," Vanessa said forcefully.

"You're arguing with yourself," Taylor observed drolly.

Vanessa exhaled a sigh of exasperation. "That's because I don't know what to believe. I don't even know what I *want* to believe."

Taylor navigated the car into a left turn lane. "Help me look for Phelps Realty coming up on the right. Should be about three blocks down. Maybe this Mrs. Phelps will be able to shed some light on some of our unanswered questions."

Vanessa sighed and pressed her forehead against the window, then concentrated on reading the signs identifying the various businesses that lined the street. "It's a long shot, isn't it?"

Taylor reached across the console and guided her chin up with his forefinger. "Chin up, kiddo! If she doesn't have any answers, we'll just find them somewhere else."

Phelps Realty was a traditional red brick building. Inside, wood paneling, thick carpets and a burnished wood reception desk projected an attitude of quiet affluence. Vanessa and Taylor asked for Mrs. Phelps and were tactfully informed that she would be with them in a few minutes.

They settled into the French provincial chairs that lined the wall facing the desk and declined the coffee offered by the receptionist.

Taylor sat erect, with his left ankle resting atop his right knee. *Obviously a man who prefers action to inaction,* Vanessa thought, watching him toy restlessly with the hem of his slacks. Scarcely a full minute had passed before he tilted his head toward Vanessa's and whispered, "I feel like I'm waiting on a dentist."

"I was thinking the same thing about the gynecologist," Vanessa replied.

Another five minutes passed before Teri Phelps entered the room. In her red blazer, white shirt and black skirt, she was an extension of the tone of quality and elegance in the building itself. She was a tall, slender woman with silver-gray hair of a shade and style that suggested the routine care of a fine salon. Her face had escaped the wrinkling of her fifty-odd years except for the deep laugh lines radiating from the outer corners of her eyes. She introduced herself, shook hands and then led them to her office in the rear of the building.

She gestured for them to take a seat and lowered herself into the oversize leather chair behind her desk like a monarch settling on a throne. "You wanted to talk about some land?" she asked without preamble. "I take it we're dealing with a specific parcel. Are you buying or selling?"

"Actually," Taylor said, "I already own this parcel. It's a parcel you used to own. You may recall Wolf Corner."

Mrs. Phelps granted him a sly smile. "Stephenson, Stephensco—I should have put the two together." After a silence that stretched too long for comfort, she said, "What exactly do you want, Mr. Stephenson?"

Taylor gave Vanessa a reassuring smile before saying, "Miss Wiggins here owns a house built on the northern edge of that property, near the site of the original farmhouse. She's curious about the property, and I've been helping her trace previous owners who might be able to tell her something of the history."

"I'll tell you anything I can," Mrs. Phelps said. "But I'm not sure what you want to know. Although my father owned that property, our family never lived there."

"It was a farm?" Vanessa asked.

Nodding, Mrs. Phelps said, "Yes. A small one, by the standards of the day. A dairy farm. But it hadn't been worked in years when my father bought it."

She smiled unexpectedly, and a faraway look softened her face. "My father wasn't much for planting and sowing, but he loved owning land. He anticipated the suburban sprawl and spiraling prices. He just didn't live long enough to reap any of the benefits. He bought a number of small farms at auction."

"Who was auctioning them?" Taylor asked.

"The Cropville Bank and Trust. The founder of that bank foreclosed on a number of farms during the Depression. Apparently everyone wondered why, since the land itself was hardly worth anything back then if no one was working it. But he had the last laugh when he brought in a wildcatter and began drilling for oil. His speculation turned out to be quite profitable."

Her eyes cut to Taylor sharply. "If you've heard rumors of oil on the Wolf Corner property, don't get your hopes up. There's not a speck of petroleum under that land. I'm surprised you didn't see the evidence of the dry holes they sank before Old Man Vandover let the land go back to the bank for auction."

"We found evidence of one exploration hole on the southeast section," Taylor said, and grinned. "We had a good laugh. The crew even called me Wildcat for a few days. But I've seen the geological data—profile's all wrong for oil or gas."

"Well, if it's not a gusher you're after, what do you want to know?"

"Did anyone live on the property after your father bought it?"

"A number of families. My father bought it planning to turn a profit renting it out. There were plenty of war veterans getting married and settling down about that time. Some of them came from farms and wanted to farm but couldn't afford to buy a place of their own. But after the first ten or twelve tenants, he'd have probably sold on easy terms to any farmer showing a keen interest and the gumption to stay."

"He couldn't keep tenants?" Vanessa asked. Her fingers curled round the smooth wooden arm of the chair as she waited on an answer.

"They kept insisting it was haunted!" Mrs. Phelps said. "Sounds silly today, doesn't it? But it was a small, rural town—if you could call a few stores, a bank and a handful of farmers a town—and you know how stories get told and embellished. A family would move in and hear the stories, and soon they were seeing ghosts."

Vanessa's hands were damp against the wood she was holding so tightly, but her mouth was bone-dry. "What..." She swallowed. "Was there a particular story connected to the haunting at the farm?"

"It was supposed to be visited by the ghost of old Mr. O'Malley. He owned the farm when the bank foreclosed on it. According to the story, the young and beautiful Mrs. O'Malley decided to spare herself the embarrassment of being evicted and packed up and ran off with a salesman who was passing through. Mr.

O'Malley was so distraught over her leaving and over losing his farm that he committed suicide."

"How?" Taylor said. "How did he kill himself?"

"You mean you haven't heard the story? That's one of the juicier parts. He got stinking drunk and hung himself in the oak tree out back."

Vanessa gasped involuntarily.

"I didn't mean to shock you," Mrs. Phelps said. "It's just an old story. I'm sure it's been embellished through the years. That oak tree was probably cut down years ago."

"No," Vanessa said. "The tree's still there."

Mrs. Phelps said, "Supposedly, O'Malley's restless because they buried him in an unmarked grave outside the gate of that old cemetery near the highway. The good, devout people of the area wouldn't allow a suicide in hallowed soil."

"My God," Vanessa said.

"Bizarre, isn't it? To think it was less than the span of a lifetime ago. Anyway, no one lived there for a long time after O'Malley died—probably not until my father cleaned up the farmhouse and started renting it out."

Taylor said, "When did the thing with the wolves start, do you know?"

"Oh, that was in the early forties, when the wolves got so thick that the state put a bounty on them. They were already calling it Wolf Corner when my father bought it."

"I thought it was called that because there were so many wolves in the area," Vanessa said.

"I'm not sure you want to hear the whole of it," Mrs. Phelps said, leveling her gaze on Vanessa.

"I'm okay."

"She can take it," Taylor said. "I'd have told her myself if I hadn't thought a history teacher would have already checked out the local color." He grinned at her, and she gave him an I'll-get-you-later-for-that-crack look.

A long silence ensued. "Well?" Vanessa prompted in exasperation.

Taylor sucked in a breath and said, "The wolves became a problem to the farmers, killing stock and frightening cattle, so the state put a five-dollar bounty on them."

"Five dollars went considerably further back then," Mrs. Phelps interjected. "Killing a wolf was a real windfall."

"In order to collect the bounty, they had to take the ears of the wolf in for proof of the kill," Taylor continued. "That left them with a carcass to dispose of, and for some reason, they began hanging the carcasses on the barbed wire fence that surrounded the abandoned farm."

Vanessa reacted with a shiver. "Why would they do that?"

"The fence was like a community bulletin board," Mrs. Phelps answered. "Most farmers passed that corner on their way into town. When there was a fresh carcass there, they had something to talk about for days. It became a local tradition."

"Wolf Corner says a lot about the area's history, the rural life-style," Taylor said. "I'd like to have a historical marker put on the corner. The county historical society sent me a whole stack of forms to be filled out. There's a lot of documentation required."

He turned to Vanessa. "I was going to mention it. I thought with your background in history, you might be able to help."

"The historical marker is a grand idea," Mrs. Phelps said. "We've lost so much life-style history to urban sprawl. The entire area will be an extension of Houston soon."

"Do you know anything else about O'Malley—his family, anything?"

"I couldn't tell you," Mrs. Phelps said. "I've told you all the story I've ever heard, and it's undoubtedly been embroidered and exaggerated beyond the most basic recognizable truth."

The intercom buzzed. Mrs. Phelps excused herself and picked up the receiver. She paused, listening, then said, "Thank you," and hung up. She rose. "I'm sorry I can't be of more help, but I've told you everything I know, and I did mention that I had an appointment to show a house tonight."

Thus dismissed, Taylor and Vanessa thanked her and left. "We've got a lot to talk about over dinner," Taylor said when they were settled in the car.

"And to think about in the middle of the night, no doubt," Vanessa predicted gravely.

They stopped at a steak house for dinner and were seated in an isolated alcove lighted by only the faintest indirect lighting and the candle in the center of their table. The low light, soft music and unhurried pace of the three-course meal provided a restful counterpoint to the confusion that had overtaken Vanessa's life since she had seen the figure in the tree. Throughout the selection of wine and entrées and a trip to the sumptuous salad bar, they chatted about her work and the antics of her students, which led to a discussion of the various rebellions of their own teen years.

"You're always talking about what a hellion you were," Vanessa said. "How did you get from being a hellion to being a successful entrepreneur?"

"Actually, Stephensco was a bribe to get me to tow the line."

"A bribe from whom?"

"My dad. After I made it through high school by the skin of my teeth, I went to work for him full-time. I had worked for him summers, and I knew the construction business inside and out—or I thought I did."

"No one is smarter than an eighteen-year-old," Vanessa said dryly.

Taylor nodded. "After a while I started pestering my dad about moving up, becoming a project supervisor. He told me if I wanted to move up, I'd have to go to college. No special treatment for the owner's son. He said I needed to learn how things worked and why they worked. Putting it mildly, I was not happy at that turn of events."

"So you stalked off and made it on your own to spite him?"

"I tried that a few months and got nowhere, of course. So the next Christmas, my dad suggested I go back to work for him *and* enroll in college at the same time. He said if I got an engineering degree and enough business training to read a spread sheet efficiently, he'd set me up in my own subsidiary."

"So you did."

"I was a rebel, but I wasn't a fool. It had occurred to me by then that I was getting nowhere trying to punish my parents for getting a divorce. I went to school, and then I started Stephensco, a subsidiary of Stephenson

Enterprises. Wolf Corner is my first project since breaking away from the Stephenson umbrella."

"Was it a friendly split?"

"Oh, sure. My dad was proud as punch when I bought out his interest."

For nearly an hour, they had set aside all thought of Wolf Corner and the ghost in Vanessa's backyard. When the waitress cleared away their dinner plates and poured coffee for them, however, it seemed almost as though she'd flicked a switch that brought Wolf Corner back to the center of their attention.

In the silence that followed the woman's departure, the O'Malley ghost became a presence at the table—not a physical manifestation as it had been in the crude gallows of the tree limb, but a presence just the same, alive and preeminent in their minds. Vanessa took a tentative sip of the steaming coffee and found it still too hot to drink. Putting her cup down, she said, "There's no doubt anymore, is there?"

"We know who it is now. We have a name, a starting point for investigation, a general time period."

Vanessa's frustration was evident in her voice as she asked, "What good is it going to do us to investigate?"

Taylor reached for her hand and covered it with his own. It was warm, and his touch was gentle. "Knowledge is power," he said.

"Does that apply to ghosts? Do *any* rules apply to the supernatural?"

She was very close to tears, and Taylor felt ineffectual because he had no pat answers to give her. If they had been alone he would have held her close to him and stroked her hair and kissed her, but he had to settle for giving her hand a reassuring squeeze. He continued holding it tightly, demanding her attention. "You said he was appealing to you for help. Maybe we can find out what he needs."

"And lay him to rest?" she asked almost in challenge. "Maybe he just wants to be inside the cemetery gate with a tombstone inscribed R.I.P."

"Maybe. And maybe it's not that simple. Don't you think you ought to try to find out?"

"You're going to nag me into it whether I do or not, aren't you?"

"Damned straight!"

For a few seconds they glowered at each other, then Vanessa smiled unexpectedly. "There's nothing more irritating than being nagged by someone who's telling you what you wish you could ignore."

Taylor grinned back at her, and the sudden tension that had sprung up between them dissolved into a comfortable silence as they finished their coffee. Vanessa traced the rim of her empty cup with her forefinger, staring thoughtfully at the dregs of coffee in the bottom, then set the cup and saucer aside. "I appreciate your support, Taylor, the way you've been there when I needed a friend."

Settling his cup in the saucer carefully, Taylor said, "It's more than friendship, you know. I'm not without ulterior motives."

Only Taylor could have said it that way, with just the right amount of levity to prove he wasn't too serious but with a bedroom leer that proved that he was serious enough. Vanessa felt color rising warmly in her face in response to the explicit hunger that shone in his eyes.

In the intimate recesses of the restaurant, it was easy to forget the way the equilibrium of her life had been disrupted during those few minutes on Saturday night. Temporarily freed from the unsolved riddles and unanswerable questions of the universe, she was free to enjoy normal, human pleasures, and the heated gaze of this man was indeed a source of human pleasure. Counterpoint to the macabre reminder of death and suffering that had invaded her home, his gaze, so earthly and male, made her feel alive and feminine.

She closed her eyes, drew in a deep breath and exhaled it slowly, savoring the contentment of being there with him. She felt his hand cover hers again, warm, strong, gently caressing, and she raised her fingers to thread them through his, savoring the resultant sense of unity, and opened her eyes.

His thumb began a slow, rhythmic massage of the fleshy area between her thumb and forefinger. The movement was sensuous, erotic, mesmerizing. She would have felt uncomfortable showing her response in bright light, but in the glow of the candlelight, she didn't try to mask the effect his touch was having on her.

And Taylor noticed—very definitely, he noticed. His voice was husky. "Men have sacrificed entire kingdoms to have a woman look at them the way you're looking at me."

"I don't want to leave," she said, and he knew what she meant. Here she'd been safe. And for a few minutes, they'd managed to shake free of the specter haunting her. "He's going to be with us again as soon as we go through the door."

"He's with us again already," Taylor said grimly.

Later, in the car, Vanessa said, "I keep thinking of what Mrs. Phelps said. The words she used—'less than the span of a lifetime ago.' When you think about it, it's not unreasonable to think that there could be someone still living who might remember the O'Malley suicide."

"An old-timer from the area?"

Vanessa nodded. "The Friends of the Library are compiling a local history, and one thing they're doing is finding elderly people who've lived here a long time and recording interviews about life-styles and historical events. Karen's been trying to get me involved. I could ask her for names."

"Good idea," Taylor said. "I was thinking of written records, like O'Malley's death certificate, but the information there would be sketchy, even if we found it."

It was almost ten by the time they reached Wolf Corner again. Taylor parked in Vanessa's driveway, then turned to her and asked, "Would you like to walk over to my house for a glass of wine or Irish coffee?"

Vanessa shook her head. "I'm going to call it an evening. I didn't get any sleep Saturday night, and *someone*, who shall remain nameless, kept me up half of Sunday night watching movies, then woke me up at the crack of dawn yesterday morning and then came over last night and stayed until midnight again."

"Ingrate," Taylor teased. He seemed to understand without asking that he wasn't going to be invited into her house, either, and he didn't push. After kissing her rather chastely at her front door, he gave her hand a reassuring squeeze. "Remember that I'm less than a block away if you need me."

Vanessa pulled her hand from his to cradle his face and stood on tiptoe to give him a fleeting kiss on the mouth. "Thank you. For everything."

She felt muscles flexing under her palm as he clinched his teeth and heard him inhale sharply as his arms snaked around her waist to pull her into a bear hug. "So help me, Vanessa, I'm going to get that damned ghost out of our lives if I have to hold a séance and dance naked under a full moon."

Vanessa might have laughed at the absurd image if he hadn't been so serious; instead, feeling a surge of tenderness for him, she pulled his face down to hers again.

He let her set the tone of the kiss, tightening his arms around her when she pressed closer to him, parting his lips when she teased them with her tongue. When she lifted her mouth from his to nibble tiny kisses along his jaw and down his neck, he growled sensually and slid his hands up her back to knead her shoulders.

"Good night, Taylor," she said regretfully, breathless from the seductive tenderness of his touch.

Taylor left more determined than ever to dispatch with her ghost quickly.

# 7

VANESSA WAS SCARCELY in the door when a giant yawn overtook her. She hadn't been exaggerating or making excuses when she'd told Taylor she was tired. The sleepless nights and early mornings were catching up with a vengeance. Heaving a mighty sigh, she kicked off her shoes and dropped onto the sofa.

The last set of essays lay on the coffee table, reminding her of her duty, but the thought of tackling the hieroglyphics of student handwriting made her cringe. The papers could wait; she was going to peel her weary carcass off the sofa and crawl into bed before she fell asleep right where she was and woke up in the morning with a crick in her neck.

Rote memory drove her through the prebed rituals of face washing and teeth brushing. She had just pulled her oldest, most tattered, most beloved sleep shirt over her head and was folding back the comforter and sheets on the bed when she heard what sounded like wind outside.

The cold front that had moved in the previous day had fizzled, yielding to a humid heat, precursor of the hot, humid summer that inevitably lay ahead. Since it had been as still as death earlier, she wondered now if wind meant a storm was blowing in. Stepping to the window, she pushed aside the draperies and lifted a vane of the miniblinds. Everything appeared perfectly calm, almost unnaturally still, except to one accustomed to the peculiarities of Texas weather.

The moon was almost obscured by thick clouds, but the features of her backyard were cast into silhouette by the street lamp on the corner. The pointed tips of the wooden fence boards aimed toward the indigo sky like sharp spears held by a line of ancient warriors, and the oak tree jutted and sprawled upward from the earth like a dark beast disturbed from deep sleep. Nothing moved except the thick clouds that slid past the moon, subduing and distorting the light it offered.

Vanessa had almost decided she had imagined the wind when a streak of lightning forked down on the distant horizon and a gust of wind swooshed through the tree and pushed briefly against the window. She waited for the sound of thunder, but none came; the storm was too distant. For several seconds more she stood there, still peering through the vanes of the blind, watching the leaves of the oak tree recover from the shock of the wind like cat hairs settling after being stroked the wrong way. Then that eerie stillness of deep Texas night returned.

Vanessa let the blind fall into place and adjusted the draperies, then crawled into bed, releasing a sigh as the mattress yielded to the weight of her body and the smooth percale sheets cocooned around her. Within minutes she was sleeping like a baby. . . .

*The mantel clock was ticking loudly, regularly, in a cadence very close to the beating of a human heart. At the window, the curtains swayed gently in a breeze that carried the scent of the climbing roses, which were in full bloom. She was content, happy, and she hummed a hymn as she stirred the soup simmering on the stove. Then, a sudden apprehension filled her. The song stuck* in her throat like a physical thing, and her eyes went to the window, confirming her fears.

The figure was large, dark, ominous. She recognized its menace. It was coming into her house, but she didn't try to stop it. She couldn't stop it; she could only fear it, hate it, because she knew what it was. The full menace of it surrounded her, stripping her of contentment, of dignity.

The figure spoke, mocking, laughing. She stiffened her spine against it and pressed her palms over her ears to block out the awful mockery as the menace advanced on her.

Powerless against it, she fought anyway. Her heart beat furiously, ripping at her chest. Mustn't let it touch her! She fled, running with all her strength, yet she could not escape. It touched her. Pain shot up her leg, excruciating, intense.

The mantel clock bonged, joining the shrill scream that tore from her throat. A strange buzzing from outside the window roared in her ears. She lunged away, ignoring the pain, refusing to yield to it, but the menace caught up with her.

The window. Light flooded through the window, mocking the dark menace. The light beckoned her. Though weighted by the menace, she turned toward the light. Pain racked through her, but she ignored it as she concentrated on reaching the light. And then, in the light, there was another figure, this one small and without menace. She froze at the sight, the realization. A piercing wail came up from her chest, then another and another, blending with the clock's ticking, the buzzing.

*The menace impaled her. She felt the defilement as it moved inside her. It sickened her. Moaning, she looked at the light, at the face in the light....*

Vanessa sat up straight in bed, clutching her chest against the violent thunking of her heart. The features of the room began falling into perspective, but knowing she was safe did nothing to allay the terror that held her in its grasp. Wrenching the bedding aside, she ran wildly through the darkness, down the long hall, until she reached the living room. She fumbled with the desk lamp, finally knocking it over, but managed to get it turned on. She didn't bother picking it up while she looked for Taylor's number on the pad next to the phone.

*Answer. Answer. Dear God, please answer....*
"Taylor?"
"I'll be right there."
The line went dead but she held on to the receiver as though it were a lifeline in a roiling ocean. Her heart still thundered painfully in her chest. The antique clock on the mantel chimed and she started and inhaled sharply, painfully, so that the air made her shudder as it passed over her raw throat. The humming of the telephone jarred her.

How long did she wait for him? She couldn't have said whether it was seconds or days, except that the clock had not finished chiming eleven times before a loud knock caused her to toss aside the telephone receiver and dash to open the door, cursing at the frustration of having to fumble with the dead bolt and chain locks.

Flinging open the door, she literally leaped into Taylor's arms. Her fists caught his shirt, bunching the cloth into an iron grip as she clung to it and pressed into the reassuring strength of his body.

"Vanessa? What is it? What's wrong?" he asked.

"Dr-dream," she said brokenly. "Aw-awful." And then, clinging to the strength he offered, she succumbed to the sobs she'd been holding at bay.

Taylor managed to get inside the house and nudge the door closed with his shoulder, then wrapped his arms around Vanessa. He stroked her back and murmured comforting phrases, but she was inconsolable. Finally he lifted her into his arms and carried her to the sofa. He sat and cradled her in his lap, soothing her until the sobs subsided. Then he brushed the hair off her face and kissed her temple. "I'm going to get you some tissues," he said. She nodded comprehension, but still, he dropped another kiss on her forehead and added reassuringly, "I'll be right back."

He returned with tissues and a damp cloth and waited patiently while she blotted and blew before sitting down next to her and laving her face with the cloth. If Vanessa hadn't been so enervated from the sobbing she'd already done, she might have cried from the sheer sweetness of the act and the gentleness with which he ministered to her. She gave a final sniff and said, "I'm not usually such a baby. It's just—I've never had nightmares before, not like this, and it was so . . ."

She leaned forward, sliding her arms around his waist and pressing her cheek against his chest. "I woke up and heard screaming again, but . . ."

She lifted her head and looked up at his face. Her eyes were limpid and held traces of terror. "It was my voice. I was the one screaming. Oh, God, Taylor, do you think it was me last time? It was so real then, and I don't remember dreaming. I just heard the screams and woke up. I was so sure . . ."

He guided her head to his chest again and stroked her hair. "There's no reason to believe the two incidents are related. You've had some bad shocks now that you hadn't had then, including hearing those screams. Maybe tonight your mind was re-creating what it heard."

"I am afraid, Taylor. What if I'm losing my mind?"

"You had a nightmare. After what you saw and what you learned today, what sane person wouldn't?" He let her ponder that idea, then asked, "Do you remember what you dreamed?"

"It was the same as last night." She said it as though it surprised her; she'd just realized herself that the dreams were similar.

"A clock and a window?"

She nodded against his chest. "Only it was more real, and I was more a part of it. Last time it was like I was watching a movie, but this time it was like I was part of it. There was something dark, something awful . . ."

"What?"

"I don't know. I couldn't see it. I just . . . It was after me, and I couldn't get away."

"Try not to think about it anymore," Taylor said, combing his fingers through her wildly disheveled hair. He was acutely aware of her as a woman, of the female scent of her, the softness of the worn knit shirt she was wearing and the feminine curves beneath. There was something aphrodisiac about being needed by a beautiful woman.

She snuggled more closely against him and sighed softly. "Feeling better?" he asked, and she nodded. He kissed the top of her head. "We could make Irish coffee again."

She hesitated before answering. "If I made cocoa instead, would you stay for a cup and maybe talk awhile?"

"Sure," he said, thinking it would take a stick of dynamite to get him to leave.

Disengaging herself from his embrace, she stood and suddenly looked down at the battered sleep shirt she was wearing. "Maybe I should . . ."

"That would be a little silly, wouldn't it? I've already seen it and you in it. Besides, it's no skimpier than a beach cover-up."

Although she abandoned the idea of putting on a robe, she didn't seem entirely convinced by his argument, and he didn't blame her. They both knew she wasn't wearing much underneath. Neither of their shirts had been thick enough to mask the pressure of her breasts compressing without restraint against his ribs. And the elastic edges of her skimpy bikini panties were well-defined under the soft knit fabric. He noticed them as she walked ahead of him to the kitchen. Even after his gaze followed the backs of her bare legs from mid-thigh down to her voluptuous calves and woman-slim ankles, it returned to her hips and those teasing ridges disrupting the smooth line of her shirt. He'd been wrong when he'd told her she had a great behind; it wasn't just great, it was world-class. He wanted to touch those malleable mounds of flesh so badly that his hands tingled with the frustration of deprivation.

Curling them into fists, he observed Vanessa's crisp, efficient movements as she worked, noting the cool confidence with which she opened and measured and stirred. Once she had combined the ingredients, she looked up at him while she continued pushing a long-handled wooden spoon around the saucepan.

"I don't have any marshmallows," she said apologetically. "I don't particularly care for them, so they're not something I keep on hand."

"I can take or leave them," Taylor said, although he dearly loved a mountain of marshmallows on top of hot chocolate when he drank it.

"I have graham crackers," she said, as though she were slightly embarrassed to admit it. He saw why a few seconds later when she took the box from the pantry; the graham crackers were shaped like teddy bears. Eyes narrowed, she cast him a warning glare.

He threw his hands in the air and shrugged. "I didn't say a thing."

"You grinned," she accused.

"I do a lot of grinning around you. I'm an absolute grinning fool when I'm around you. I think it might be love."

This time, she did the grinning. "You're as punchy from lack of sleep as I am."

"It could be insanity induced by sexual frustration," he speculated.

"The world would be filled with grinning faces if that were the case," she countered.

"So," he said. "You're feeling better."

"It was just a dream. I overreacted." She studied the curlicues the spoon made on the surface of the cocoa as she stirred the chocolate for a minute or so and then looked at Taylor. "Have you ever had a bad nightmare."

"No. But I had a roommate in college who'd been in a terrible automobile accident. He used to wake up screaming." He stepped closer to emphasize his point. "His terror was real, Vanessa. So was yours."

"Did he practically knock you over and cry on your shoulder?"

"No. Once he woke up, he recovered quickly. He would remember that it wasn't happening again, that it was just a dream."

"You mean if it keeps happening, I'll get used to it?" Vanessa asked as she leaned across the range to turn the burner off before the cocoa boiled.

"Umm," Taylor answered. The tail of her shirt crawled perilously close to the bottom edge of those round cheeks that kept preempting his attention. He held his breath, then watched with keen disappointment as the shirt fell back into place when she straightened.

"All in all, I'd just as soon not have any instant replays of tonight's feature presentation, thank you," she said, oblivious to his preoccupation. Abruptly she turned and opened the cabinet where she kept cups and drinking glasses. One mug was on the edge of the second shelf, easily accessible, but all the others were on the top shelf. She stood on tiptoe and stretched, but her fingers still couldn't reach the handle.

The tail of her sleep shirt crept to within a quarter inch of the elastic edge of her panties. Taylor sucked in a breath and held it in an effort to control the effect the sight was having on his central nervous system and assorted portions of his anatomy.

Vanessa made another lunge for the cup and missed. Releasing the air in his lungs, Taylor made the magnanimous sacrifice of forcing his eyes away from the tail of her shirt in order to step forward and play gentleman. "Here. Let me...."

His voice trailed off as his throat suddenly went bone-dry. For, as he'd stepped forward, Vanessa had stepped back, and this fortuitous combination of opposing actions had brought his crotch into direct collision with her backside.

The nightshirt, the flimsy little bikini panties he'd been imagining, the zipper in the front of his jeans might as well have not existed. They might as well have been buck naked as they brushed together that way. The current of sexual desire that jolted through Taylor vibrated from his scalp to the tips of his toes and buzzed every nerve ending in between. He would have forgotten his name if asked for it at that moment. He was too aware of Vanessa to remember anything, to register anything beyond sensation. She turned toward him, and the shock that shone in her eyes told him she was as smitten by the sexual excitement that had arced between them as he was.

He thrust the fingers of his right hand into the wild tumble of her hair and snaked his left arm around her waist to pull her against him. An erotic whimper of anticipation rose from her throat as their bodies pressed together.

Coaxing her head back by delving deeper into her hair, he let his eyes feast on the sight of her face as she waited for his kiss. Her lips parted with a sibilant whisper of invitation. She was looking at him the way she had in the restaurant, with that combination of innocent awe and nubile yearning. A slight twist of his wrist positioned her face perfectly, and he dipped his head to brush his mouth lightly, briefly over her lips to test their taste and texture, afraid if he allowed himself too much, too soon that he would lose what tenuous control he still maintained over his emotions.

The intensity of his desire for her scared him just a bit; he was a virile man with normal needs, but he'd never been quite so obsessed by any woman as by the woman he now held pressed to his body. It was a multifaceted obsession; desire seemed to carry with it an inherent responsibility, almost an entrustment of her welfare, as though care was a toll demanded for fulfillment.

Having accustomed himself to the velvet lushness of her lips, he brushed his mouth over hers in slow, rhythmic passes until she pressed upward, subtly demanding more. He made an involuntary sound—equal parts gasp, groan and sigh—and then answered her sweet demand with the urgency he'd been holding in check. Fusing his mouth solidly over hers, he deepened the kiss. She welcomed the advance with the tightening of her arms around him, the pressing of her body even closer to his. He lowered his hand—finally—to cup the glorious curve of her bottom, sliding the fabric up with his palm until his fingers splayed over bare silken skin and warm satin.

The cabinet was only inches behind them, and he backed her against it, trapping his hand between the wooden panel and her pliable flesh, forcing her aching softness against his heated hardness.

The frank intimacy of that sudden cradling revealed to her in detail the immediacy and degree of his arousal. The intimate knowledge sent a stab of answering excitement radiating through Vanessa. She gasped into his mouth at the startling intensity of it.

Taylor broke the kiss and eased away from the counter, grudgingly relinquishing the intimate contact with her. The fingers entwined in her hair combed their way to the ends. "You didn't call me here for this."

"Are you so sure of that?" she asked hoarsely. "I'm not."

He stared, transfixed, at her face. Her cheeks were flushed, her eyes bright, her lips still imprinted with the pressure of the kiss. For a fleeting instant he wondered how he was going to resist taking advantage of her. Her beauty stole his breath away—and her vulnerability grabbed his integrity by the lapels and reminded him of the fatal flaw in his character: decency.

"You would be an hour from now," he said bitterly, forcing himself to turn away from her. Damn it, but life was unfair to decent men.

Though he couldn't see her, he was aware of her movement behind him as she filled the mugs and put them on the tray she'd prepared, then walked out of the kitchen. He took in a shuddering sigh and released it, then followed her to the breakfast nook.

Vanessa's hands were trembling so hard as she raised her mug of chocolate to her mouth that she wondered how she'd managed to get the tray to the table without sloshing cocoa all over the place. The scene in the kitchen seemed less and less believable as she tried to sort out what had happened and how it had happened so fast.

She didn't say anything when Taylor sat down in the chair across from hers and picked up his mug. In fact, neither of them spoke for a while. Taylor opened the box of graham crackers and dumped a handful onto his napkin. He'd eaten a few of them when Vanessa reached over to snitch one from the stack. Some of the tension between them dissolved as their eyes met, and they exchanged smiles over the absurdity of two adults sharing bear-shaped crackers in the middle of the night after very nearly making love on the kitchen counter.

The tension subsided but the silence remained. Vanessa's mind tumbled over and over in circles of thought that took her from the terror of her dream to the automatic reflex of calling Taylor to the strong attraction that had sparked between them. He'd said that in an hour she'd be sure again why she'd called him; at the moment she couldn't think of one thing in the world that she was sure of, except that she never, ever wanted to have another nightmare like the one that had roused her tonight. She wasn't even sure whether the shakiness that still plagued her was a lingering effect of the nightmare or the kiss or a combination of the two.

They'd finished their cocoa when she mused aloud, "It was the same dream." Taylor straightened in his chair, letting her know he was listening.

"Last night and tonight," she said. "It was basically the same dream, only more detailed this time." She paused thoughtfully. "I've never had a recurring dream before."

"Does it have any special significance to you?"

"The window part is easy. Yesterday I opened the windows when I got home from work, and when the cold front blew in, I closed them, yet it was still drafty. That's when I decided to call customer service. It was on my mind when I fell asleep."

"And the clock?"

"I thought . . ." She hesitated, debating whether she should tell him her clock theory.

"Thought what?" he prompted.

Oh, what the hell? she decided. After the way she'd responded to his kiss, she had little to lose. Life was full of gambles, anyway. "I had been... I was hoping you'd come over, and just before I fell asleep, I checked the clock and it was nine o'clock and I was disappointed that it was so late because I thought . . ."

"That no respectable gentleman would come calling that late?" he suggested.

He was too smug for Vanessa's comfort, and she frowned at the pleasure that showed in his face. "No respectable gentleman would," she parried, and smiled a saccharine smile.

"So that's why you were so hostile," he teased. "Thought you'd been stood up!"

"We didn't have a date," she snapped.

"Then why were you all gussied up?"

"I . . ."

"You had on that fancy dress and that ribbon in your hair and that perfume. . . ."

Vanessa poised her mouth for a fresh denial but decided to surrender graciously in the face of defeat. "Guilty," she said.

"I'll be damned!" he said, punctuating the expletive with a smug chortle of laughter.

Vanessa suppressed the urge to tell him to please do exactly that. Instead, she said, "That's irrelevant. Anxiety over a drafty corner and a . . . *minor social disappointment* would not motivate the type of terror-filled dreams I had tonight."

"Freud could probably find a connection," Taylor said wryly.

"I should have known you'd bring him up!" Vanessa said.

A silence followed, then she asked softly, "Do you think I need that kind of help? A psychiatrist?"

Taylor's lips compressed into a hard line as he pondered the question. He took his time answering and spoke guardedly. "Only you can make that decision."

"That's a cop-out answer."

"I can't make a decision like that for you."

"You could give me your opinion."

"All right. You want an opinion, I'll give it to you: You saw a ghost, and it shook you up—enough to give you some freaky nightmares. I'd say that makes you perfectly sane, with healthy coping mechanisms."

He must have read the gratitude in her eyes, because he got up from his chair abruptly and reached for her hand. "Come on. Come sit with me on the sofa." When she hesitated, he said, "I just want to hold you."

They sat much as they had earlier, with Vanessa leaning across his chest to rest her head on his shoulder. He was solid and warm and strong where she touched him, and it was heavenly to surrender herself to that strength. Cuddled next to him, she felt safe, totally invulnerable.

But safety was not the only feeling he evoked in her. The small of her back was wedged against his upper thigh and the resultant warmth was not all accountable to the combining of the trapped heat of two bodies. She remembered vividly the hard bulge she'd felt straining against the front of his jeans, the sensation of his fingers pressing into the smooth flesh of her buttocks, the flames of desire that had licked up inside her when he'd fit that hardness against her.

She remembered, too, as she relaxed against his chest, how automatic it had been to dial his number, knowing he would come to her. *Knowing.* It seemed just as automatic to cradle his face in her hand now and raise her head to kiss his cheek and then smile at his surprised expression.

"Thank you," she said.

"Is that a specific thank you or a generic thank you?"

"Generic, I think."

A silence followed, then Taylor said, "You can go to sleep if you like."

"This isn't fair to you. You've got to get up early in the morning—earlier than I do."

"I couldn't sleep anyway if I left you alone. I'd be too worried about you, wondering—"

"Taylor?"

"Hmm?"

"You were right earlier. That wasn't why I called you."

A muscle flexed in his cheek, and she felt the sudden tension that overtook his body, and for the first time she considered how difficult it must have been for him to turn away from her. He'd never tried to hide the fact that he was attracted to her, but she'd always considered his sexual bantering to be mostly typical male hyperbole, small talk of the heterosexual bachelor.

*They'd fit together so perfectly.* The thought, a very vivid tactile memory, sent heat coursing through her. She felt it spreading upward from her chest to stain her cheeks with a blush and down to areas that were uniquely female, igniting a need that reminded her she was a woman. She tried to say his name, but her mouth had gone dry, and she had to swallow to moisten it before trying again.

He looked down at her. "Hmm?"

"That wasn't why I called you, but I . . ."

He'd been stroking her hair away from her face soothingly, and he stopped abruptly in midstroke. "Go to sleep, Vanessa. We've already had the discussion."

She raised her palm to his cheek to force his face toward hers. Her eyes met his unflinchingly. "It wasn't why I called you, but I need you that way now."

His body tensed again noticeably, but before he could respond, she slid her arms around his neck and tucked her forehead against his breastbone. She talked to his chest, as though her appeal might filter through to his heart. "You make me feel warm and alive and human. Please, Taylor, I desperately need to feel all those things tonight."

She both heard and felt his heartbeat accelerate as he hugged her urgently and buried his face in her hair. "I'm only human, Vanessa. I couldn't turn it off again. Don't ask me for something you're not sure you want. If this is your misguided way of saying thank you . . ."

Their eyes met again as she tilted her head back. "If I just wanted to say thank you, I'd bake you chocolate chip cookies."

The knowledge of what they were about to share settled over them. They savored it as they continued looking at each other. The solemn sweetness in Taylor's expression made Vanessa want to cry. The various needs that had led her to ask him to stay were confused and inseparable, but key among them was Taylor himself. He took her seriously; he was taking the prospect of making love to her seriously. That mattered to her.

The silence, at first thrilling and meaningful, stretched overlong. Vanessa turned her face away from his and said softly, "I use a contraceptive sponge for birth control, but I don't have—"

"I have one in my wallet."

She nodded, then straightened to a sitting position with her back to him, hating the awkwardness. "There's a basket of guest toiletries in the front bathroom. Just make yourself at home. Unless you were planning to go back to your house. . . ."

The weight of his hand unexpectedly came to rest on her shoulder. "I'm not leaving you alone in this house tonight. I told you that. Not even for five minutes."

Unable to trust her voice, she simply nodded. A tremor of emotion passed through her. He traced the length of her arm to her wrist, encircled it with his fingers and tugged gently, urging her back into his embrace. She let her shoulders fall against his chest and sighed as his arms went around her and crossed above her breasts.

"I'm an extraordinarily lucky man," he said.

"An extraordinarily *nice* man," she corrected.

He kissed her temple. "Lucky," he said firmly. After a pause, he added, "Meet you in your bedroom?"

Vanessa rolled her eyes. "I don't believe this! An assignation."

His arms tightened. "Uh-uh. No backing out."

"I wasn't backing out," she said. "It's just so aw—"

"Vanessa."

His voice was authoritative, so uncharacteristically stern that she swallowed the rest of the sentence in a gulp. Cupping her chin in his right hand, he tilted her face up, then twisted so that his face was above hers. "I'm going to kiss you now, and you're going to kiss me back. And then you're going to get up and go to your bedroom and get ready for bed . . . and for me. And you're not going to be embarrassed or insecure, because you're a beautiful woman and I want you at this moment more than I've ever wanted any woman in the whole of my life. Now, have we communicated?"

He was teasing, yet the way he looked at her left no room for doubt about his sincerity. She felt as though she might laugh and cry at the same time. "Oh, Taylor!"

"Sh," he cautioned, letting the fusing of their lips cut off the admonition. Thus began a deep kiss that reminded Vanessa why she'd invited him to stay and celebrated her good judgment in doing so. When he released her, she leaned her head against his shoulder and closed her eyes against the dizzying effects of passion, trying to regain enough composure to move. She wasn't quite sure her legs would work if she stood at that moment, and she knew she couldn't see straight.

Apparently Taylor was as afflicted by the passionate malaise as she, because it wasn't until his breathing had returned to near normal that he said, "You really do kiss good when you're in the mood."

"Oh, I wasn't *really* in the mood," she said, perversely mischievous.

"Liar!" Taylor said, pinning her back against his chest. Voice rich, tone sensual and suggestive, he cooed into her ear, "Didn't you have somewhere you were going to go and something you were going to do?"

"That was when I *was* in the mood."

"Maybe I can get you in the mood again," he persuaded, nibbling at her neck.

"Not a chance."

"Oh, yeah?" he asked, lifting her hair away from her ear so he could nip at her earlobe.

"Well, maybe a slight chance...."

"Just a slight one?" Taylor asked before tracing the rim of her ear with his tongue.

Involuntarily, Vanessa sucked in a lungful of air. "Maybe better than slight."

"How much better?" he asked, devoting his attention to her neck again.

Vanessa wrenched away from him and stood up, then gave him a beguiling smile. "Better enough to remind

me of where I was going and what I was going to do."
She gave him a parting smile before leaving the room,
knowing his eyes were following her as she walked and
feeling imminently desirable because of it.

The confidence of desirability went with her into the
bedroom. As she freshened up in the vanity-bathroom
that was part of the master suite, she heard the gurgle
of running water from the front bathroom and smiled.
She'd always found sharing bathrooms and wash-
basins a bit awkward, and she would have been self-
conscious sharing the most intimate areas of her living
space with Taylor just yet. But knowing that he was just
two walls and the space of a small room away, also
primping and priming, heightened her anticipation
without making her feel as though her privacy were
being invaded.

Anticipation, she decided as she switched on the
bedside lamp, surely was the world's most potent
aphrodisiac.

The sheets on the bed were badly askew, an unwel-
come reminder of the nightmare that had awakened her
earlier. Vanessa pulled them straight and folded the top
sheet over the edge of the handmade quilt invitingly,
then slipped between the sheets. Although an uneasi-
ness remained with her when she recalled the dream,
the terror that had wrested her from sleep and sent her
dashing from the bed had abated in the face of time,
perspective and Taylor Stephenson.

As though she'd conjured up his image, Taylor appeared in the doorway. He'd taken off his shirt, and for
the first time Vanessa saw the chest that she had come
to know through touch. A sprinkling of caramel-
colored hair formed a T that tapered into the waistband of his jeans. She wondered briefly whether the

hair would be coarse or soft to the touch and then looked up at his face. The expression in his eyes took her breath away.

He sat down on the far edge of the bed and leaned toward her, bracing his weight on one arm. Never taking his eyes off her face, he said, "You don't have any idea how desirable you are, do you?"

"You shaved," she said, lifting her hand to smoothe the backs of her fingers over his cheek.

"I found a disposable razor in the basket."

Vanessa smiled and patted the pillow next to hers, then folded back the edge of the top sheet. "It's late. Why don't you get into bed."

"A man could wait a lifetime on an invitation that sweet," he said, dipping forward to drop a brief kiss on her lips before standing up to take off his jeans. Reaching into his pocket, he pulled out a foil pouch, which he slid under the pillow. Then, checking to make sure she was watching, he gave her a smile steamy enough to melt a glacier and reached for the button at the waistband of his jeans. The heavy zipper made a grating sound as he opened it. Looping his thumbs over the waistband of his jeans, he shoved them down over his hips and stepped out of them. He left them where they lay on the carpet, then did the same with his briefs.

Not once did he turn away from her, and not once did Vanessa's gaze leave his body. The overall leanness of him, the aesthetic perfection of the configuration of male muscles, held her in thrall. Her eyes trailed the pattern of hair to his navel and then lower, where it led to the parts of him that differed so drastically from her own body. He was partially erect and already impressive.

"Just from looking at you, thinking about you," he said, following her gaze. He smiled. "Now you know what you do to me."

Self-conscious suddenly, Vanessa closed her eyes and snuggled deeper into the mattress with a motion that was unintentionally seductive. She heard the soft rustle of the sheets and felt the lurch and bouncing of the mattress as he sat, then stretched out under the covers beside her.

Taylor rolled onto his side and propped his weight on his elbow, then touched her face with his forefinger, urging her to open her eyes. When she did, their faces were just inches apart. Satisfied to have her attention, he slid his hand from her cheek to her neck and then across her shoulder and down her arm to her hand.

Vanessa's self-consciousness evaporated as he traced her fingers with his forefinger as though he adored them, each one of them, simply because they were a part of her, then lifted her hand to his mouth to kiss them one at a time.

The need for words evaporated along with her self-consciousness. This was Taylor; she knew this man—his patience, his strength, his compassion. The warmth of his body lured her, and she surrendered willingly to the gravity pulling her toward the depression his heavier body made in the mattress.

He rolled back, freeing his arm so he could slide it under her neck as she settled against him. Her knee touched his thigh, and her toes slid down his shinbone. A subtle movement brought the length of their bodies into full alignment. Taylor reflexively tightened his fingers around hers and guided their entwined hands under the sheets. He opened her hand and pressed her palm against his chest. The sensitive nerve endings of her fingertips registered the coarseness of the caramel-colored hair about which she'd speculated minutes before. Exploring the hair-sprinkled muscles, Vanessa discovered a nearly flat nipple and kneaded it, relishing the growing rigidity her ministrations produced.

Taylor breached the hem of her shirt to glide man-rough hands over her ribs, then to the small of her back and down to the plump swell of her buttocks. In response Vanessa crooked her knee across his thighs and undulated closer to him. Shoving the tail of her shirt up under her arms, he readjusted his weight on the mattress and, draping his arm across her ribs and splaying his fingers over her back, drew her flat against him. The hair on his chest chafed her sensitized breasts, teasing them to a warm, aching fullness. Moaning softly, she strained closer to him.

Taylor finessed his thigh between hers and also strained closer, pressing swollen male flesh—hot and hard—with voluptuous female flesh—soft and pliant. A sound of passion rasped from Vanessa's throat. "That's what touching you does to me," Taylor whispered intensely, cradling her bottom and anchoring her tighter against him.

Vanessa combed her fingers into his hair, trapping his face under hers, then nibbled over his freshly-shaved cheeks before nipping at his lips to coax his mouth open for a soul-wrenching kiss. She was aware of every place their bodies touched, of the contrasting textures of their skin and hair, of the need building inside her in response to the imposing evidence of his need throbbing against her stomach.

Without sundering the contact of their mouths, Taylor rolled her onto her back and covered her body with his. Supporting his weight on one elbow, he levered slightly to the side so he could gather her breast in his free hand. He kneaded it with his fingertips, flicked his thumb over the taut nipple, rolled it lovingly between his thumb and forefinger, then soothed it with his palm. Vanessa arched her back convulsively. The single motion gave him freer access to her breasts and caused her stomach to rub against his erection, drawing a sharp groan of sensual pleasure from him.

Vanessa gasped as well and reached between them to touch him. She circled him with her hand, tightened her fingers around him. His flesh lurched in response, and she felt an answering spasm deep inside herself. "I want you inside me," she said.

"Here?" he asked, sliding his finger inside her.

Her breath caught at the sudden burst of sensation. She couldn't answer him; breathing had become too much of a chore to allow her to speak. But her body answered by thrusting upward against the heel of his hand.

Taylor buried his head between her breasts and flicked his tongue over her skin, tasting it while he inhaled the scent of her perfume, and felt the slight quivering of reaction. His groan was equal parts aroused male growl and frustration. "I think it's time for responsibility," he said.

Vanessa sighed her disappointment as he drew away from her and rolled over. She closed her eyes and burrowed her head into the plumpness of the pillow, still aware of his body near hers, feeling its warmth, smelling his scent, hearing him draw ragged breaths into his lungs. The foil yielded with a metallic click, and the muffled whisper of the condom being uncoiled followed. And then, finally, the mattress shifted as Taylor returned to her.

Trailing kisses along the ridge of her jaw, he ran his hand over the length of her arm until he encountered the sleeve of the sleep shirt. He laughed softly as she hastily pulled off the shirt and tossed it aside.

"Impatient?" he teased, letting her gentle nudging coax him atop her. This time his penis brushed the spot that had thrust against his hand earlier, and the expression that flitted across her face answered the question beyond speculation.

"Turn out the table lamp," she said when she was capable of speech, and Taylor did so.

Darkness added a new dimension to their lovemaking, heightening their remaining senses by depriving them of sight. Perfume, after-shave, man, woman blended in the air they breathed. Skin, hair, roughness, smoothness, hardness, softness—all the textures were there for their appreciation. Each intake of breath, each sigh of encouragement, each whispered admonition fueled their desire.

Their mutual need built until they were beyond words and logic, and ultimately their bodies united in a single delirious thrust. They moved together slowly, frenziedly, furiously. There was an affinity to their being linked, a rightness. Vanessa clung to Taylor, arched her body toward his, moved with him. She was the first to climax, and when the world began falling away around her, she held fast to Taylor as though he alone could save her from shattering into fragments. Her hands clasped almost punishingly around the muscles that crisscrossed his shoulders, her legs locked around his hips, pressing ever closer to him.

The contractions of the female muscles surrounding him, Vanessa's intense cry of ecstasy, the urgency with which she clung to him all drove Taylor toward his own release. Her cry had been an extended sigh, his was a guttural growl: male and female reactions to the ultimate union and shattering physical fulfillment. They lay together, boneless, depleted, sated, while their lungs recalled how to breathe normally and their hearts slowed to a normal rate. Urgent grasps eased to gentle caresses.

Taylor said her name as a question, and she opened her eyes to admire his face above hers. "Just don't leave me," she said. "Don't let go of me yet."

"I couldn't move if the bed was on fire," he assured her.

"It isn't?" she asked, finding the energy to smile.

"Not anymore," he said. "But it was a raging inferno for a while there." He lifted her hand and pressed her palm to his lips, held it there for several seconds, then placed it against his chest, as he had at the beginning of their lovemaking. "You are . . ."

"I'm what?" she prompted, after the sentence had hung unfinished for what seemed like a very long time.

"Probably getting squashed," he said, carefully separating his body from hers so that he could lie beside her instead of atop her.

"I hadn't noticed," she said, and sighed as he pulled her back against him and wrapped his arms around her.

Perhaps a minute later, he said, "I've got to get up, just for a minute or two."

Vanessa made a sound of regret that was part "oh" and part "ah," then perversely snuggled closer to him and ran her toes down his shin, intentionally making it difficult for him to leave.

The sound he made closely resembled her nonword, but as if to prove his strength of character, he dropped a kiss on her temple and pushed up on one elbow. "Got some housekeeping to do," he said. "I'll be back in two minutes."

"One," she bargained, using a feminine, almost feline wiggle to unfair advantage.

*Cropville, Texas—1945-46*

DANNY BANNERSON TOOK A ROOM at the Widow Shugart's boarding house and found a job with Cropville's only construction company. He courted Jessica a respectable period of time, and they were engaged a year before getting married in the Cropville Bible Church. He drove the automobile on their honeymoon trip to Houston, where they stayed at the Rice Hotel.

Jessica was pathetically inexperienced with men on a personal basis. Respectable women saved themselves for marriage, and until Danny entered her life, she had never met a man interesting enough even to tempt her to do otherwise. She was carried across the threshold of their suite a nervous bride very much in love with her groom.

Danny nursed a martini in the hotel bar while Jessica bathed in scented water and then put on a lace and satin peignoir set. Then, cleansed, perfumed and cloaked in the finest lingerie available in the growing city of Houston, she paced the floor, waiting for her husband.

Waiting to become his wife in every sense of the word.

# 8

TAYLOR WOKE UP with a snowflake in front of his face.
At least, when he was still half-asleep, it looked like one
of those plastic snowflakes people decorated with at
Christmas. Another degree of wakefulness enabled him
to identify it as the hand-crocheted lace that edged the
pillowcases on Vanessa's bed.

*Vanessa.* His mind involuntarily reverted to the evening before as his body began registering sensory details—the smoothness of percale sheets, the scent of
Vanessa's perfume, the pleasant warmth of her body.

She was lying spooned against him, with the top of
her shoulder wedged under his left arm. His right arm
was across her waist, loosely embracing her. The top
of her head was just inches below his nose, and several
strands of her hair had fallen across his chest and become tangled in his chest hair. The toes of her left foot
were tucked under his knee. The tail of her shirt had
ridden up, and her bottom, that delightful, plump female bottom, was pressed against him.

Taylor lowered his right hand to cup her right flank
possessively and smiled. The sheer pleasantness of
waking up in this cozy bedroom with Vanessa next to
him was overwhelming. It filled him in a way that was
almost physical, as though contentment were a liquid
nourishment that could be poured into the vessel of
human need.

As the weight of his hand settled on her hip, Vanessa stirred, made a feline cuddling motion that pushed her bottom even more snuggly against his ribs and sighed softly. Taylor wrapped his arm around her waist again and scooted closer to her. Within seconds he was wishing he'd packed a spare condom in his billfold. He considered the feasibility of throwing on his jeans and dashing home to raid his medicine cabinet before Vanessa woke up, but nixed the idea as too chancy. What if he got back and she was already awake and out of bed, thinking he'd ducked out on her? He decided to stay exactly where he was.

Contentment and the lingering effects of a sound night's sleep had left him enervated, but it was a psychologically healthy lethargy, a state of mind where he acknowledged that, as nice as the promise of making love again was, being there with Vanessa cuddled up against him was nice, too.

As if sensing how appreciated her presence was, Vanessa sighed again, more awake than before, and Taylor was glad he hadn't left. He didn't want her waking up and discovering him gone. He'd promised not to leave, and he wanted her to know he was a man who kept his promises.

Unable to move without the risk of disturbing her, not really wanting to move anyway, he lay still, noticing details of the room's decor. A framed needlepoint sampler with a sentimental verse about home and hearth hung on the nearest wall, and he wondered if she'd done the needlework herself. The thought brought a smile to his lips. Needlepoint. She was the type. He'd bet the profit on a house in Wolf Corner that she'd handpicked or handmade or could have told him a personal anecdote about the history of every item in

the room. The sepia-toned faces staring at him from
oval wood frames undoubtedly were relatives, great-
grand-somethings-or-other. Had one of them made the
quilt draped over the quilt rack at the foot of the bed,
or had she found it at some quaint little antique shop?

Though the mattress was an innerspring, the bed-
stead itself was old. The head and foot rails were tu-
bular iron that had been painted with white enamel.
The ceramic washbowl on the chest of drawers was
cracked with age, and he wondered if the large brass
spittoon, now the adopted home of a well-tended and
lush philodendron, had once actually been used as a
spittoon, or if it simply was a replica suggestive of the
era when spittoons were routinely used.

Curious about the bric-a-brac of her personal life, he
speculated about the treasures hidden in the half dozen
or so ornamental boxes that surrounded the ornate silver hand mirror on her dresser. Jewelry? Hair combs?
*Tie tacks that had belonged to former lovers?* The
thought gave him pause. He didn't like thinking of Vanessa with another man.

Puzzling over the sudden surge of jealousy, he turned
his attention away from the dresser and tucked his
forehead against the back of her head. Her hair brushed
silkily against his skin. She had beautiful hair. It could
be called brown, but at close range it was a combination of colors from rich chestnut to golden maple. And
it smelled mysteriously female, the way a woman's hair
should smell. It was the kind of hair a man could spend
a lifetime touching and smelling. But then, Vanessa was
the kind of woman a man could spend a lifetime discovering.

It came to him in a blinding flash of revelation that
he wanted to do just that: spend a lifetime discovering

the woman lying next to him in bed. He was in love with Vanessa.

He lay still, letting the realization and its ramifications sink into his conscious mind. There should be trumpets sounding fanfare or fireworks exploding or sirens going off, he thought. But there was just the quiet comfort of Vanessa's bedroom, the cozy softness of her bed, the gentle sound of her breathing. Somehow, they were more significant than pomp or hoopla.

Taylor had always thought falling in love would be a gradual process, that he'd come to want commitment and permanence and all the attendant accoutrements by degrees as a relationship progressed. But that was before he'd taken the plunge. No wonder they called it falling! It was like leaping from an airplane at thirty thousand feet—and he'd landed on a cloud-soft bed of percale and lace with a woman who smelled like heaven. Pretty heady stuff for a sensible man of thirty-two.

Pushing up on his left elbow, he took his right arm from around her waist to lift the hair off her neck. He kissed it, then blew gently in her ear. She groaned a sleepy protest. He kissed the tender skin behind her ear, then blew in it again. Her response this time was a longer groan, accompanied by a twitch of her shoulders. Smiling at his own impatience, he dropped his head back against his pillow, draped his arm around her waist again and cuddled up next to her to wait for her alarm clock to go off.

He watched her grope for the clock when the shrill alarm sounded, fascinated by the expressions on her face as the noise sank unrelentingly into her peaceful sleep to rouse her and amused by the uncharacteristic clumsiness of her sleep-impaired movements. His attention focused on her face as he waited for her to become aware of his presence and remember the night before. The emotions were as plain as day—realization, remembering, smiling acceptance. He'd never thought her more beautiful than when she blinked at him and smiled and said, "You did stay."

He dipped to kiss the tip of her nose. "I told you I would."

Cuddling up to him, she said, "I'm glad." Her eyes widened. "This is late for you, isn't it? I'm not making you late for work, am I?"

Drawing her to him in a bear hug, he said, "Go ahead—make me as late as you like. I own the company, remember?"

"That's very tempting," she said, and sighed contentedly. "This is very nice."

Taylor indicated his agreement by kissing her temple.

"Unfortunately," she said as though she really felt it *was* unfortunate, "I don't own the company I work for, and if I made you late, I'd be making myself late, as well."

They were silent a moment, then she said, "Taylor?"

"Hmm?"

"Thank you. For coming when I needed you, for holding me, and . . . for staying."

"You needed me."

"But you didn't have to get so involved."

"Of course I did."

She became aware of where his hand had roved without his even realizing it. "Because of my great behind?"

"Because I'm madly in love with you."

Vanessa closed her eyes and made a groaning sound. "It's too early in the morning for hyperbole."

"Hyperbole?" Taylor was crushed. He'd been so sincere—couldn't she see how sincere he was? Couldn't she hear it? Wasn't she *feeling* it too? How could she possibly *not* feel it?

Everything he was thinking and feeling was written on his face. Soberly, Vanessa said, "You weren't ser—" She half laughed, as though she'd just caught on to a joke. "Taylor, please cut this out. You're a morning person, but I'm not up to clever repartee at six-thirty."

He was too distracted to worry about protecting his ego. "It's not clever repartee, and it's not hyperbole, and I *am* serious," he said, outraged. "You can't trivialize love, Vanessa. It's a natural force. Like gravity. Or centrifugal force."

"I'm beginning to think you *are* serious," she said, as nonplussed as he was. His face assured her he truly was. She pulled herself up into a sitting position. "Please don't do this, Taylor."

He sat up, too, facing her directly, and looped his fingers around her wrists, demanding her attention. "Something happened last night, Vanessa. Something special."

"Yes," she said tenderly. "It was special for me, too. I needed you desperately and you were there, and I clung to you because you were understanding and caring and reassuring, and I'll never forget how reassuring it was to have you here."

It seemed to Taylor that she was being deliberately obtuse. His grip on her wrists tightened imploringly. "Damn, Vanessa, don't you feel what's going on between us? I want to wake up with you every morning for the rest of my life."

Vanessa groaned. "Oh. Heaven help me. I've got a ghost in my tree and a romantic lunatic in my bed."

Taylor yanked her hands forward and up so high that her fingertips were touching his chin. "If I'm a lunatic, it's because you turned me into one. You're beautiful and sweet and you've got a great behind and you smell wonderful, and you've got snowflakes on your pillow-cases and—"

"It was your first time," Vanessa said, disbelieving the situation. "You were the world's oldest virgin bachelor and you got carried away last night, and now you think you're in love."

"Please don't make fun of me, Vanessa. I've never felt this way or said these things to a woman. And I wasn't a virgin and you damned sure know it!"

The air drained from Vanessa's lungs in a rush. "I can't deal with this now."

"Get dressed and I'll take you to breakfast. We can talk about it after you've had coffee."

"I don't mean now, as in this minute, I mean *now*, when I've got a ghost haunting my tree and I'm having recurring nightmares."

He guided her hands to his shoulders, then slid his hands up her arms to her shoulders. His eyes fixed on hers, holding them captive by their intensity. "I love you."

He thought for a moment she was going to cry. Vanessa feared the same thing. He was a virile, vital, sexy man, and the way he was looking at her was so . . . potent . . . that surely any sane, sensible woman still drawing breath had to be a fool not to melt into his arms when he told her he loved her.

She didn't melt into his arms, exactly; she merely sagged forward until her forehead lodged against his breastbone, then groaned.

"THIS WASN'T WHAT I had in mind when I offered to buy you breakfast," Taylor complained as he opened a fast-food container to take out a breakfast croissant.

"We didn't have time for flambéed bananas at Brennan's. I've got to be at school in twenty minutes. These are good. Ham, eggs and cheese. Real stick-to-the-ribs stuff."

Taylor's seemingly noncommittal "Um" conveyed a lot of editorial comment.

Vanessa ate half of her croissant, then abandoned it. "Taylor..."

"Don't say my name in that tone of voice. It makes me feel like I'm back in high school."

"I'm sorry if I spoiled what you thought would be a special moment."

"'Special'?" he asked, his voice dripping satire. "A man tells a woman he's madly in love with her—why should that be special?"

Vanessa winced at the bitterness in his tone. "Last night was...*wonderful*," she said softly, reaching across the table to put her hand on his. "I just don't think right now is the time for either of us to be making any...life significant decisions."

Taylor scowled at her. "'Life significant decisions'?" He harrumphed, then picked up the croissant she'd abandoned and took a bite.

"Everything's all jumbled up, Taylor," she said. "What happened between us *was* intense, and I would never have asked you to stay, you know, after I got calmed down, if I didn't care for you. But I don't know how much of the intensity was chemistry between us and how much was some crazy aftershock from having been so terrified and having someone strong and wonderful to hold on to."

"There's nothing jumbled up about what I'm feeling."

"How can you be sure of that? Look, Taylor, I'm not naive. You didn't just happen to jog by on that Sunday because you were attracted to me or because you were concerned about me specifically."

"I was—"

"You were concerned about Wolf Corner. I was incidental, because I was the one who'd called the cops in the middle of the night. You wanted to know what was going on so you could take care of it."

"The ruthless developer. Nothing counts but the bottom line. Is that what you think of me?"

Vanessa gave a sniff of exasperation. "I'm not painting you as some heartless, money-grubbing capitalist. Why shouldn't you be concerned about Wolf Corner? I've heard you call it your baby." She paused to scowl at him. "What are you grinning about?"

"A 'heartless, money-grubbing capitalist'?"

She decided to ignore him so as not to encourage him.

He said, "I love it when you used those cockeyed phrases. I love *you* when you use them. You're not only beautiful, you're cute."

"You didn't get really interested in me until this past Sunday," she persisted. "Not until I was so upset over the ghost. You took care of me. You gave me wine, Taylor, and you listened to me...."

"I was plotting how to seduce you."

"You like being needed."

"Everybody likes being needed."

"You like it a lot, Taylor. It's part of your personality. And I've leaned on you. I've been so very needy. How can you be sure that at least part of what you're calling love isn't just your attraction to my need?"

"Because the needs you fill in me go beyond my being needed."

"If that's true, then we don't have to be in any hurry, do we?" Vanessa said.

"I'm thirty-two years old, Vanessa. This isn't a crush or an infatuation. I feel as though I've fallen off the edge of a cliff."

"You've only known me in extraordinary circumstances. I'm not going to be in a crisis state forever. Sooner or later I'm going to come to grips with my ghost and my fears. Why don't we wait and see how you feel about the self-sufficient Vanessa Wiggins before you make any broad proclamations?"

The set of Taylor's jaw was rigid as he drew in a ragged breath. "You're not going to close me out in the interim," he warned. "We're not going to pretend we never met or that we never made love."

"That would be silly, wouldn't it?"

Taylor gave her a look that said, "Damned right it would be silly," and a silence stretched between them.

"I've got to get to school," Vanessa said finally.

"YOU SAY THIS OLD MAN knows everything that's gone on in this area for the past eighty years?"

"According to Karen, he's the mother lode of local history," Vanessa told Taylor. "Almost ninety years old, with near total recall. She says the tapes they made of him for the oral history at the library are phenomenal."

"This could be our turn coming up. See if you can read the name on the mailbox."

"Dahlmann. This is it."

A packed earth road led them to a frame house. A trio of rockers were lined up on the porch that spanned the entire front of the house, and in the one nearest the door sat an elderly gentleman wearing a white undershirt and dungarees held up by wide suspenders.

The ancient dog lying at the man's slippered feet, a shepherd blend whose muzzle had grayed with age, lifted his head from his paws as Vanessa and Taylor stepped onto the bottom step, then rose grudgingly, stretched his stiff hind legs and gave a token half bark.

"Mr. Dahlmann?" Vanessa asked. "I'm Vanessa Wiggins. We talked on the phone."

The man dropped a hand to scratch the dog behind the ears. "Settle down, Gus. This here's a teacher lady. She's not going to hurt nobody."

Gus gave her a wary look and then plopped down and emitted a wheeze that sounded uncannily like a sigh.

Dahlmann's face had the weathered texture of wrinkled leather, but his eyes shone with intelligence. He fixed one of those eagle eyes on Vanessa. "This your gentleman friend?"

"This is my neighbor, Taylor Stephenson," Vanessa said. "He built the houses at what used to be Wolf Corner."

"That so?" Dahlmann asked, pinning Taylor with a vexed look. "Well, sit down, anyway. Take a load off." He spread his arm to indicate the free rockers.

Vanessa and Taylor sat as instructed. "You want to talk about the wolves?" Dahlmann asked. He didn't wait on an answer before continuing. "Used to always be a wolf or two on that fence. Hung a few of 'em there myself. Hell—excuse my French, ma'am, but I'm an old man, and I talk the way I like—one night Otto Stokes and I got liquored up on corn liquor and almost shot Gus's grandmother, thinking we had us a wolf."

His face was animated now, his eyes shining with memories. "It was late January and cold as blue blazes. We was going to take the five dollars to the livestock show and have us one good time. Lucky for old Gus here, Nell—that was my wife's name, Nell—stopped us, or old Gus here'd never've been born."

Dahlmann shook his head, suddenly somber. "She was a good woman, Nell. Been gone nearly twenty years now. Died of cancer, real slow. No woman should have to go that way."

Before Vanessa could couch an appropriate sympathetic response, Dahlmann said, "Still miss her."

There was a silence, which provided a natural opening to change subjects. "Mr. Dahlmann, we're interested in the farmer who used to live on the farm at Wolf Corner. O'Malley. Do you remember him?"

Dahlmann pondered the question a moment. "Paddy O'Malley? Yes, I knew him. Knew Tilly, too. She and Nell visited sometimes, gossiping and doing women things. Always seemed like a decent Christian woman. Wouldn't a believed it of her, running off like that. But she was a pretty little thing, and I guess if she got a notion that she wanted to run off, it wouldn't a been too hard finding a man who'd let her run off with 'im. They'd had some hard times that year. Some mighty hard times."

"What kind of hard times?" Vanessa asked.

"Things was pretty bad all over. We'd all had a hard year. Too little rain, so things was lean for all of us.

Paddy's well dried up, and he had to haul water out to the stock and the fields. Then Paddy broke his leg. Had to hire a man on to help. Didn't have enough money to hire someone after the bad year before, but he had to hire someone if he wanted to keep the place going, so he went to the Cropville Bank and Trust, and Old Man Vandover give him a loan to hire a hand and put in a new well."

He harrumphed. "Old Man Vandover gave a lot of loans like that. He knew O'Malley wouldn't be able to pay back that loan on time, but he give it to him any-way. Times was bad, and everybody thought Van-dover was some kind of saint. Until the notes came due and he wouldn't extend on 'em. Paddy would have been able to pay him back after another good year, but Old Man Vandover wouldn't listen to nuthin' or nobody."

The rungs of Dahlmann's chair creaked on the old wood of the porch as he rocked methodically back and forth. "They was desperate at the thought of losing their land," he continued. "Hell, they didn' have nowhere else to go."

"So Tilly O'Malley ran away?"

"That's what they all said. Nobody never heard hide nor hair of her after it all happened, but the suitcase was missing. There'd been a salesman through town, a smooth talker. He'd asked a bunch of questions about her up at the store, so folks put two and two together when she disappeared at the same time he did."

He shook his head. "I'd a just never believed it of her. Maybe a woman'd leave a man when times are bad, but it was a real shocker, her leaving her little girl like that."

Taylor and Vanessa exchanged surprised looks. "The O'Malley's had a child?" Taylor asked.

"A girl," Dahlmann said. "Maggie was her name. Saddest thing you ever seen. Came home from school and found her papa hanging there. Never quite got over it, from what I hear."

"What happened to her?"

"She didn't have nobody left, what with her mother run off like that and her daddy dead, and no relatives to speak of. She went to live with the Widow Hanks in town. Went to work at the five-and-dime when she was old enough. Worked there until it closed back 'bout ten years ago. Far as I know, she never got married."

"Is she still alive?" Vanessa asked.

"I ain't heard no different, but I don't get around much no more to talk to people." He harrumphed. "Hell, ain't nobody left to talk to, if I could get around. Most everybody I knew is dead."

"Is there anyone who might know where I could find out what happened to Maggie O'Malley?" Vanessa asked.

Dahlmann's rocker ceased its creaking as he planted his feet flat on the floor to think. "I reckon any of the Morehouses would know. They ran the five-and-dime. Mr. Morehouse ran the store until he died, then his girl, Betty, and her husband took it on. The boy's name was Staal. Henry Staal. They still live on the old Morehouse place, out on the farm-to-market. If anybody could tell you about Maggie O'Malley, they could."

Dahlmann resumed his rocking. Gus growled in his sleep and his hind foot slid across the board floor of the porch in a dull scrape before he settled into deep slumber again. Vanessa took a small notebook and pen from her purse and wrote down the names Dahlmann had given her, then asked, "Have you heard anything about Wolf Corner being haunted, Mr. Dahlmann?"

"Been haunted for years," Dahlmann said matter-of-factly. "Folks 'round here didn't take kindly to a man killin' hisself, 'specially when he's all liquored up. Either way, he ain't in no state of grace. They buried him outside the cemetery. Maggie, she raised all kinds of a ruckus 'bout that, but right is right. After that, folks started seeing O'Malley out in that tree, just the way Maggie found him when she come home from school that day."

"Did they ever consider moving the grave?"

"No, ma'am, they didn't. Maggie tried to convince 'em for a long time, but she finally give up, and after that, guess there was nobody to care in partic'lar. Ain't nobody lived out there at Wolf Corner in years, till they moved in and built all those matchboxes."

He rolled those sharp eyes in a gesture of disdain. "Sub-dee-visions. People living right on top of each other. Got houses so close together nowadays that they hear each other snoring at night."

Leaning forward for emphasis, Dahlmann fixed a hawklike glare on Taylor. "Sorry if I'm hurtin' your feelings, son. Can't help the way I feel. Sub-dee-visions. People on top of each other. Can't no good come from that."

With a shuddering wheeze of breath, he slumped back in his chair. "Anythin' else you want to talk about?"

"I think we've covered it all," Taylor said wryly as he and Vanessa rose to leave.

"Thank you for seeing us, Mr. Dahlmann," Vanessa said, reaching down to shake hands with the elderly farmer. "You've been very helpful."

Back in the car, Taylor commented, "Quite a character."

"Sharp as a tack," Vanessa agreed, then added somberly, "He must be lonely, living alone, with his wife and all his friends dead. Karen said he flatly refuses to leave his house and go somewhere where he could be around other people."

"He didn't seem to think much of the idea of living around other people," Taylor said.

"Did his attitude bother you?"

"I'm a developer, Vanessa. I've heard it all before. Given his age and perspective, I'm surprised he wasn't harder on me than he was. He worked the land all his life. It must seem to him that I'm blaspheming everything he worked for."

"O'Malley had a daughter. Mrs. Phelps never mentioned her."

"Do you suppose she's still alive?"

"Dahlmann didn't say how old she was when it happened, but he indicated she was a child."

"Which means she would be somewhere in her sixties."

"I want to find her. So far everything we've heard has been third person. I'd like to get her account of what happened to her father. Any idea where the 'old Morehouse place' is?"

"There're still a dozen old places around here. Did you get the other name?"

"Mm-hmm. Phonetically. I'll have to find everything close in the phone book and start calling." She was quiet a moment, thinking. "Are we anywhere near the old cemetery?"

"Going grave hunting?"

"We've still got some daylight. Are you game?"

"The lady's wish is my command. But don't expect too much. The cemetery's in pretty bad shape. I don't know if we'll be able to find anything there."

The cemetery bore out his pessimism. Weeds grew with profuse liberty in cracks in the strip of unkempt asphalt that served as a parking lot, and the iron fence was in disrepair, its gates unevenly suspended on worn hinges and its slender posts coated with rust. Vanessa and Taylor walked the entire perimeter outside the fence searching for evidence of O'Malley's unmarked grave and found nothing more significant than broken beer bottles and decaying plastic cartons that had once held fast food.

When they had come full circle, Vanessa stared at the rust-covered letters set into the fence that identified the area as a cemetery and frowned.

"Disappointed?" Taylor asked superfluously.

She sighed. "I thought we'd find something to indicate a grave—a mound, a depression, a pile of rocks. You'd never know a man was buried here. It makes you wonder how many unmarked graves there are. We could be standing on one."

The thought made her shiver. Taylor spread his arm across her shoulders and gave her a gentle hug. "Come on. Maybe we'll find something inside."

Some of the tombstones provided interesting reading, but most bore only names and dates. Many were weathered beyond legibility, some toppled or crumbling. In the steamy warmth of early Texas evening, the desolation of death hovered over the disheveled graves like a suffocating mist. Sensing its unsettling effect on Vanessa, Taylor said, "Let's get out of here. The sun's almost gone."

He drove to a restaurant that catered to young singles. Gaudy and raucous with rock music, animated conversation and spirited laughter, it was an excellent counterpoint to the doom and gloom of the graveyard, and they were both in a more positive frame of mind by the time they reached Vanessa's house.

"That's strange," Vanessa said as they stepped into her living room from the entry hall.

"What is?" Taylor asked, intrigued by the perplexed expression on her face. He could watch that face forever and never tire of its many variations.

"I can *still* smell the roses in here," she replied. "I threw them out this afternoon because the scent was absolutely cloying. You'd think—"

"I'm not thinking about roses," Taylor said, pulling her into his arms. "Do you know how many hours it's been since I kissed you?"

"Three," Vanessa calculated. He'd kissed her very thoroughly before they'd set out for Mr. Dahlmann's house.

"The three longest hours of my life," Taylor said as his mouth lowered to hers. He kissed her hungrily, crushing her body into his by tightening his arms around her waist, growling his impatience for the ultimate joining of their bodies as his mouth plundered hers as though he might devour her.

He hugged her tighter still, lowering his hands to cup her buttocks and press her against his swelling hardness, and dragged his mouth off hers to kiss her neck and follow the neckline of her blouse to the point where the top button frustrated his quest for the taste of more of her flesh. "It just gets better and better with you," he rasped, his chest heaving as he struggled for breath. "How could it get better?"

Straightening, he sucked in a ragged lungful of air.
Though he loosened his hold on Vanessa, letting his
arms slide back up around her waist, he maintained
contact with her by peering directly into her eyes. "I
came triply prepared this time," he said. "Let's hope it's
enough. Right now, I just want to get you to the bedroom before we decide to test how uncomfortable three-
quarter-inch carpeting can be when it's spread over a
half-inch pad on a concrete slab."

HOURS LATER, Vanessa shoved up on one elbow to look
down at Taylor's face. "I think you should go home tonight," she said.

"If I were capable of moving, and if I wanted to go
anywhere, it wouldn't be anywhere without you,"
Taylor said. They were in Vanessa's bed, arms and legs
entwined, exhausted and utterly complacent. They'd
made love twice, first with the same urgency as the
night before and then less hurriedly, taking their time,
discovering new pleasures and subtle nuances in their
loving and touching.

"I mean it, Taylor. We can't . . ."

"Can't what?" he said, grasping a few strands of her
hair and brushing his face with the ends as though they
were a paintbrush.

"Cohabit."

He mustered enough energy to roll his head so that
he could nuzzle her neck. "We're doing it beautifully."
He dropped a loud kiss on her neck. "Wonderfully."
Another kiss and a deliberately sensual sigh. "Satis-
fyingly. Let's make it official. My house or yours?"

"Be serious, Taylor," she said, making a less than
determined effort to pull away from him. "It's too soon,
and I told you I can't make any—"

"'Life significant decisions,'" he finished for her.

She succeeded in getting to a sitting position. "Don't make fun of me, Taylor. I'm not ready for this kind of involvement."

"You were ready enough about an hour ago."

Vanessa crossed her arms over her chest atop the sheet she'd wrapped around her breasts. "Don't confuse the issue with sex. We may have a high sexual compatibility quotient . . ."

Taylor rolled his eyes in exasperation. "My God, Vanessa. 'A high sexual compatibility quotient'?"

"You're trying to change the subject."

"Do you have a dictionary of convoluted phrases to pop out in the middle of heated discussions?"

"You're not listening. You're deliberately—"

"How do you calculate a sexual compatibility quotient?" he challenged. "Where do you get the numerical values to create a quotient out of something as subjective and intimate as sexual compatibility?"

Vanessa dropped back onto the pillow and pulled the sheet over her head and groaned—not a sound tactical maneuver considering that most of Taylor was already under the sheet with her. He simply ducked his head under and put it on the pillow next to hers and, with his forefinger, guided her chin toward him until they were eye-to-eye. "It doesn't make any sense for me to leave. We've already tasted the forbidden fruits."

Vanessa chuckled. "We had more than a taste. We had a virtual smorgasbord."

He took heart in the touch of humor. "It isn't just sex between us, Vanessa."

"I know that!"

"Then why—"

"I don't want you in my bathroom!"

"There's another one down the hall."

"You've got an answer for everything, don't you?" she said, scowling.

"I don't have the answer to why we're lying here with the covers over our heads arguing."

Vanessa had been holding the top edge of the sheet in a death grip. She flipped her arms down, taking the sheet down, too, so that their heads and shoulders were uncovered. "Because you don't listen. I'm just not ready for the kind of involvement that includes spending entire nights together, and you're going to have to accept that."

He rolled away from her and punched the mattress with his fist. "Women!" Then, slapping a hand over his heart dramatically, he said in a mocking falsetto, "You don't care about me. All you want is sex. You don't ever want to *stay* and just be together afterward."

"Obviously that was another woman!"

"It was every woman I've ever heard complaining about men, that's who it was. And I have to fall in love with the one woman in all of civilized society who wants me to leave after earth-shattering, mind-blowing, all-consuming sex."

"Now who's got a dictionary of convoluted phrases?"

"Now who's avoiding the issue?"

"You're crowding me," Vanessa said.

"I can't help it. I love you."

"It's not that easy or that quick for me. I can't be blissfully independent and unattached one week and then totally committed the next, especially when there's so much going on outside of our relationship."

"Aha!" Taylor cried triumphantly, waving a finger in the air. "You admit we have a *relationship*."

"If we didn't, Taylor Stephenson, you wouldn't be in my bed buck naked in the afterglow of earth-shattering, mind-blowing, all-consuming sex!"

He pushed up on one elbow and flashed a grin that could have gotten him arrested for impertinent smugness—and unfair sex appeal. "You like me, Miss Wiggins. Admit it!"

"More than like," she admitted, forcing the words through a suddenly tight throat. "Oh, Taylor, I do care about you, and I love being with you, but I'm so confused. I'm flattered that you think you're in love with me and that you want to stay with me, but I won't be pressured into something I'm just not ready for. And please quit looking at me that way. I'm only human and you're sexy as all get out, and you're taking unfair—"

He cut her off with a kiss, not the probing, demanding kind, but the sweet, understanding, caring kind. When he raised his head, severing the contact of their mouths, and looked down into her face, she could see love and regret and understanding in his eyes. "You always seem to be able to appeal to the better side of my character. Good night, sweetheart. Sleep tight. And remember that I'm only a telephone call away."

For some perverse reason, the victory saddened Vanessa rather than relieved her. "Taylor..." she said with a sigh.

Taylor was already out of bed, pulling on his pants. He shot her one more look. "I'm only human, Vanessa. Say one more word and I'm not going to be able to leave, and at least one of us will end up hating me in the morning." He grabbed his shirt and pulled it on without bothering to button it, then stuffed his socks into his pockets and shoved his bare feet into his shoes.

"I'll make sure the front door is locked behind me, but I'd feel better if you promised to put on the chain locks."

*Houston & Cropville, Texas—1946*

JESSICA HAD FELT the tease of passion as Danny courted her. With her limited knowledge of all things sexual and reproductive gleaned from a pristine book on human sexuality and the chance witness of a pair of dogs mating in her backyard, she had fantasized about their honeymoon and the consummation of their marriage. Her fantasies, softened by the romance of an innocent imagination and intensified by the normal tension that mounted between a man and a woman during a prolonged courtship, were pretty pictures framed in gilt. They played in her mind like scenes from a romantic movie, accompanied by the swelling notes of orchestral music that crescendoed as they reached that mystical, magic moment that people always dreamed about.

Wearing the virginal white peignoir she'd bought on a trousseau-shopping trip in the city, she stepped into Danny's open arms. He kissed her the way he always had, and she melded against him, offering herself to him.

The kiss went on and on, just like in her fantasy. She thought it would never end and prayed it wouldn't. She was hot and curious and anxious to learn the secrets of womanly fulfillment. When Danny's tongue prodded her lips, urging them open, and pushed into her mouth, she opened to him and felt a new, mysterious surge of energy fill her, exciting her, urging her to push closer to him in a way that would be shameful if he wasn't her husband.

*So this is it*, she thought, her mind providing the music. *So this is what it means.*

Danny urged the robe of her peignoir off her shoulders and kissed her neck while he scrunched the tail of her gown in his hand until he was able to reach under the hem and touch the side of her thigh.

That sweet, fleeting touch was like an appetizer set before a starving man. It whetted his appetite while intensifying it. A sensual growl rose in his throat as he greedily slid his hand along the silken length of leg.

It was several seconds before his brain registered the sudden rigidity of her body, and even then the significance of it evaded him. In his aroused state, it took a strong shove against his chest to make him fully aware that Jessica no longer was acquiescent to their lovemaking. Dumbfounded, he said, "Jessica?"

Cheeks still flushed from their kiss, Jessica stood opposite him, gasping for breath. "Jess?" he asked.

"I . . . You surprised me," she said.

He embraced her again, tenderly. "I'm sorry, Jess. I just want you so bad I forgot to go slow. I've waited so long, baby. So long."

"I know. I want . . . I won't panic again."

But she did panic. She panicked every time he tried to touch her where no one had touched her before, tensing, shoving Danny away from her. After several demoralizing attempts at lovemaking, she burst into tears.

Danny held her and stroked her hair and comforted her as he might a distressed child. "It's been a long day, with the wedding and all. Let me hold you tonight, and when we wake up, it'll be a whole new day."

But a new day didn't help. Nor did returning to Cropville and familiar, comfortable surroundings. It was ever present between them: Jessica's stark, unrelenting terror when they tried to consummate their marriage.

Jessica remained apologetic, Danny remained patient and reassuring, but the strain tore at them. It was a churning volcano that erupted again and again during the weeks that followed.

"I'm sorry. I'm so sorry, Danny. I thought it would be different this time," became a litany Jessica chanted as tears streamed over her cheeks.

"You think it's going to be different every time," Danny said sadly. "But it never is. Jessica, I love you, honey. I want to make love to you."

"I know," she said. "And I do, too, but—" She sniffed. "Let's try again, Danny. Please. I won't pull away this time. I—"

He let out a growl of frustration. "You're too upset. Hell, Jess, I'm too upset now. Here, just let me hold you. I can't stand to see you cry."

"How can you love me?"

"I love you because I love you."

"But how long can you keep loving me, when..." The end of the sentence was buried by a muffled sob. "When I can't be a real woman for you?"

Danny sighed a defeated sigh. "I'm just going to have to love you for as long as it takes, I guess."

# 9

EARTH-SHATTERING, MIND-BLOWING, all-consuming sex and sleepless nights take their toll even on the most virile of men. Sheer physical exhaustion caught up with Taylor as he lay in bed watching the evening news, and he hit the Power Off switch on the remote control.

Although Vanessa had never been in his bed, he missed having her there. She belonged next to him, no matter where they were! He fell asleep wondering how long it would take her to realize that.

He was jarred from deep sleep sometime later by the persistent ringing of the doorbell and sprang out of bed instantly alert. *Vanessa!* Grabbing his pants, he shoved one leg in and started to the door in a gallop-hop, gallop-hop gait, trying to get his other leg in his pants as he ran.

She was on the doorstep, wearing jeans, a sleep shirt and flip-flop slippers, disheveled and wild-eyed as on the previous evening and only slightly more composed. She dashed in the moment the door opened and threw her arms around him.

"I didn't want to come," she said with her face pressed against his neck. She clung to him with a fierce, surprising strength. "It's so unfair after I sent you home, but I . . ." She threw her head back so she could see his face. "Oh, Taylor, I couldn't stay there by myself. It was so awful. I had to come."

With his hands on her shoulders, he pushed her far enough away that he could put his face directly in front of hers. "I'm here for you any time you need me. Any time. But don't you ever, ever apologize for coming to me again." He brought her back against his chest, hugging her tightly and stroking her back consolingly.

They held each other for a long while. It was Vanessa who spoke first. "We've got to quit meeting like this."

Taylor recognized the hysteria masked in the attempt at humor. "Another dream?" She nodded against his chest. He rubbed his knuckles over her cheek gently. "I'm going to get us some wine, then we'll talk."

Vanessa was curled up in the corner of his sofa, looking vulnerable and small, when he returned from the kitchen with the wine. She accepted the glass he offered and took a generous draft. "What time is it?"

"Quarter to four," he said.

"This isn't fair to you."

He slid his arm around her, tucking her shoulder under the crook of his arm. "I'm not complaining."

A silence followed while Vanessa sipped her wine slowly but persistently. When she had emptied the glass, she put it on the coffee table and said, "It was the same dream, only. . . worse."

"Worse how?"

"Longer. More detailed." Stretching her arm around him, she pressed her cheek against his chest. He felt the urgency in the way she clung to him, the fear she was trying to hold at bay. She was breathing quickly and deeply; her breasts heaved against his chest. "It was. . . more real. I. . . felt everything, and I could see. . ."

She drew in a shuddering breath and released it. Her voice vibrated with remembered fear. Or, perhaps, fear that had never really abated. "The figure at the window—I could see it this time. It was..."

The first tears came, the first sob. "Oh, Taylor, it was a little girl. I could see her plain as day. She was wearing a cotton smock with an apron, and her hair was long, and it was combed into curls, you know, old-fashioned long curls like little girls used to wear. She was staring into the room, and her eyes were...they were wide open and she was...horrified."

She swallowed a sob and raised her head. "It's Maggie O'Malley. I've written her into the nightmare. My mind is scripting this nightmare and I don't know what any of it means, except that I'm going mad."

Taylor did the only things he could do: he held her, stroked her, kissed her, whispered assurances in her ear. Half carrying her, he guided her to his bed and gave her a tissue and wiped her face with a damp cloth and then crawled into bed and wrapped his body around hers as though he could shield her from the fear that was threatening to destroy her. "You don't ever have to go back to that house again," he whispered. "You don't ever have to be farther away from me than this when you sleep."

They slept curled together until Taylor's alarm clock rang. He turned off the shrill wail and looked at Vanessa, who was sleeping so soundly she hadn't even stirred. Careful not to disturb her, he slipped out of bed. After plugging in the coffee maker, he showered and shaved. Then he went back to the kitchen and poured himself coffee and sat down at the kitchen table to drink it, thinking about Vanessa. If he'd known whom to call to report that she was too ill to come to work, he'd have let her sleep. But no one answered at the school where she worked or the school district business offices, so he filled a second cup with coffee and carried it to the bed-room.

It took a while to rouse her, but finally she opened one eye and said something that resembled, "Huh? Wha . . . ?"

"It's six-thirty," he said. "What do you want to do about work?"

The other eye opened. "Work?" She pondered the idea. "I've gotta go."

"Are you sure? Can't you call in sick, get some rest?"

"I don't . . . I never miss work."

"Can't they get a substitute?"

"It's terribly short notice."

"You need some rest."

"I couldn't."

"Yes, you can. I'll stay home, too. We'll play hooky together, sleep till noon and then rent some old movies or something."

"My classes are supposed to see a film today. If I were going to miss school, today would be a good day to be out."

"Who do you have to call?"

"The principal," she said.

"Here's the phone," he said before she could change her mind. After she hung up, he dialed his own office, and by the time he got back into bed, she was already asleep.

VANESSA STRETCHED felinely and then resettled against the seductive length of Taylor's nude body. "You're a terrible influence, Taylor Stephenson, leading me into idleness and irresponsibility."

"You forgot lasciviousness," he said drolly.

She snuggled closer. "That part I can forgive you for. But I've never skipped school before."

"I used to skip school all the time. It was never this nice."

"I feel utterly decadent." They'd slept until almost one, then made love.

"I feel," Taylor said, "like staying here forever and ever." He kissed the top of her head lazily.

Vanessa was the first to breach the long, comfortable silence that followed. "I can't do it, Taylor." The way she said it told him that her mind was inexorably made up.

"Do what?" Taylor asked, dreading what she was about to say.

"Stay here where it's so nice and safe and pretend that 16245 Howling Wolf Drive doesn't exist or that I didn't see O'Malley in that oak tree." Her eyes were large and filled with determination as they met his. "I can't run away from it."

Taylor turned his head away from her, breaking eye contact. "I never really believed you would," he said sadly.

Another silence ensued.

"I'm one payment into a thirty-year mortgage. I can't just . . . walk away."

Taylor didn't reply. After an awkward pause, she added adamantly, "It would always be dangling. I'd never be able to live with myself if I ran away and didn't try to deal with it."

"You're arguing with yourself again." The way he said it indicated he found the peccadillo utterly charming. When Vanessa didn't comment on the observation, he said, "So, where do you want to have lunch before we start trying to find Maggie O'Malley?"

"STILL BUSY?"

Vanessa replaced the receiver of the pay telephone and nodded. "First there's no answer, then it's busy for an hour."

"We're only a few miles away. Why don't we just go out there?"

"Are you sure you know where this place is?"

"If it's the one I'm thinking of, it's on that open stretch just outside of town."

The name on the mailbox verified that they'd found the Staal home. A sprawling stone ranch house had been built next to the original homesite, which was a frame, dogtrot-style house on blocks, similar to Dahlmann's.

"Looks like somebody's home," Taylor commented, nodding toward several cars parked near the detached garage.

A lanky teenage boy, all arms and legs, answered the doorbell. Vanessa explained briefly why they were there. The boy considered the information a moment and said, "I'll get my mom."

He disappeared, closing the door behind him, leaving Taylor and Vanessa standing on the porch. The teen's voice filtered through the door. "Mom?" and then, "Somebody wants to ask you something about Miss Maggie."

The door opened again, and a woman in her mid-forties greeted them with curious regard.

"Betty Staal?" Vanessa said, and introduced herself and Taylor. "We're trying to locate Maggie O'Malley. Mr. Dahlmann thought you might be able to help us."

Mrs. Staal hesitated, then stepped aside and gestured for them to enter. She led them to a den, where two preteens were seated on the floor in front of the television set, playing electronic video games that produced a series of whoops, whirs and musical flourishes.

"We tried to call ahead," Vanessa said, "but first there was no answer, and then the phone was busy."

"I have three teenagers and a preteen. The phone stays busy from two-thirty to nine-thirty," Mrs. Staal said. "We signed up for call waiting, and now they keep two lines busy at once. My husband and I finally had a separate line installed. With an unlisted number."

She indicated that they should sit on the couch and sat down in an armchair opposite them. "You said you wanted information about Maggie O'Malley?"

"I live in the Wolf Corner housing development, near the site of the old O'Malley farm," Vanessa said. "I've become interested in some of the local history, and I'd like to talk to Maggie O'Malley. Mr. Dahlmann said you might know where she is."

Mrs. Staal hesitated before answering. "Yes, I know where she is."

Misinterpreting the hesitation, Vanessa asked anxiously, "She *is* still living?"

"Oh, yes. She's still alive," Mrs. Staal said. She had pressed her hands together, interlacing her fingers, and she studied them for several seconds before turning her gaze back to Vanessa. "May I ask what you want to talk to her about specifically?"

"Her father's death."

Mrs. Staal leaned back in her chair and exhaled heavily, obviously debating whether or not to help Vanessa find Maggie O'Malley.

"Do you think she'd talk to me?" Vanessa persisted.

"Oh, yes. I'm sure she would. It's just . . . Miss Maggie's so . . . unsophisticated." She smiled. "I grew up calling her Miss Maggie. She worked for my parents before I was born and was still working in the store when we closed it down."

Her tone of voice changed subtly. "By all rights, I should feel as though she's a second mother to me. But the truth is, I feel more as though she's an adopted child. She's very vulnerable."

"I would never hurt her," Vanessa said. "I just . . . I need to know more about her father's death."

Mrs. Staal drew in a deep breath. "You've seen the ghost."

"Yes."

"Lots of people have seen it. You know, Miss Maggie never believed that her father killed himself. She thinks he comes back because . . ." She pushed a strand of hair from her forehead and sighed. "I think I'm going to let her tell you about it. Just, please, remember that she's . . . fragile."

"I will," Vanessa assured her.

"She lives in a rest home over in Katy. I'll give you the address and phone number. They have specific visiting hours, and they like you to phone ahead."

"Thank you, Mrs. Staal," Vanessa said as the older woman pressed a sheet of paper into her hand.

Mrs. Staal hesitated as though debating whether to say something, then squared her shoulders in resolution. "Miss Maggie likes plants, especially blooming plants. She keeps her windowsill covered with them. It would be a nice gesture—"

"I'll be sure to take her one," Vanessa said.

They stopped at a convenience store so Vanessa could telephone the rest home. "We can visit anytime between six and seven-thirty tomorrow evening," she told Taylor after speaking with the receptionist.

"That leaves tonight," he said. "The evening is still young. Want to take in a movie? *Nightmare on Elm Street 25?*

"I think I read that Disney is rereleasing *Bambi*."

"We'll compromise," he said, and they did, on a zany romantic comedy.

"Hungry?" Taylor asked on the way home.

"Not hungry-hungry," Vanessa said. "Eating lunch at three o'clock plays havoc on the taste buds." She leaned her head against the back of the seat, utterly content. "They should have a name for a meal that's too late for lunch and too early for dinner. Like brunch, only..."

"Dunch?" Taylor asked, chuckling. "Or linner?"

"Now we know why they don't have a name for it."

"How about picking up a pizza and then catching the evening news?"

"Pepperoni and mushroom?"

"With extra cheese."

"And Chianti."

"You're on."

Much later, after they had finished the pizza and a bottle of wine and had been cuddled together on the couch in a state of euphoric enervation through the evening news, Vanessa rolled her head against Taylor's chest and said, "I'm not going to have any nightmares tonight. I couldn't. I'm too..." A sigh completed the thought.

"Me, too," Taylor said. "Let's go to bed."

"Yes," Vanessa agreed, wrapping her arms around his neck to pull his mouth down to hers. "Let's."


THE NURSERY NEAREST the school was running a special on miniature rosebushes. Vanessa chose one covered with tiny red blossoms and had the clerk wrap the pot in red florist's foil and add a wide polka-dot bow. It looked pert and cheerful.

"She ought to like that," Taylor said when he arrived at Vanessa's house.

"I wonder what she's like," Vanessa said as they drove to the rest home. "Mrs. Staal made her sound so frail. I hope my questions don't upset her."

"Mrs. Staal seemed very protective of her. She wouldn't have told you how to find her if she'd thought your visit would upset her too much."

"I suppose not," Vanessa said.

The receptionist in the lobby of the home had them sign a log and gave them clip-on visitor tags. "We'll tell Miss O'Malley you're here. She'll meet you in the solarium in a few minutes. It's down the hall, then left. You'll see the sign."

Maggie O'Malley was neither crippled nor infirm, but she walked as though the thick soles of her shoes were weighted with lead. Her shoulders drooped in a way that said she'd been defeated by life and had long since accepted that defeat. Her face, without makeup and faded by age, was framed by a haircut as shapeless and devoid of style as the cotton dress she wore.

"You the folks who wanted to see me?" she asked, nervously pushing her thick-lensed eyeglasses higher on the bridge of her nose. They were bifocals, set in fashionless frames that did not complement the shape of her face. Vanessa thought sadly that she looked like a person who'd never had anyone to care for her and felt compassion for the child whose parents had deserted her, each in his own way. Miss Maggie from the five-and-dime: thrust out of childhood prematurely, she'd never fully blossomed into an adult, but had been trapped into a perpetual state of the adult child.

Vanessa introduced herself and Taylor and held out the miniature rosebush. "Mrs. Staal said you like plants. We brought this for you."

Maggie was noticeably moved by the gesture. Touching one of the tiny blossoms, she smiled and said, "Little biddy roses." Her speech carried the lethargy and nasal twang of rural Texas.

An awkward silence fell over them after they sat down around a game table. Strangely, it was Maggie who spoke first. "Betty sent you?"

"She told us where you lived," Vanessa said.

"How is she? She getting along all right?"

"She seemed very happy," Vanessa said.

"She always was a happy little thing," Maggie said. "How about those kids of hers? I guess they're growing like weeds."

"They were keeping her telephone busy," Vanessa said, glad to be establishing a rapport with Maggie.

Maggie chuckled. "Betty used to keep her daddy's phone busy. After Henry Staal started courting her, they was together or on the phone the whole livelong day. Even when she come to work in the store, he was hanging around her like a flea on a hound. Mr. Morehouse finally give him a job just so's Betty could get some work done. I don't reckon he ever dreamed Henry Staal would wind up running the store."

Lost in memories, she toyed with the ribbon on the flowerpot for several seconds before turning back to Taylor and Vanessa. "What'd you want to see me about?"

She went back to picking at the bow while Taylor explained the situation briefly. Maggie dropped her hands into her lap and stared down at them for a long moment. Then she raised her eyes to meet Vanessa's. "You saw my daddy hanging in that tree?" Her sadness was almost palpable.

"I don't know," Vanessa said. "I saw something, and I felt like he was asking me for help. But I don't know what to do for him. I thought maybe you could tell us something that might help me understand the situation better."

Maggie wiped her open hands over the skirt of her dress, smoothing the broadcloth over her thighs. "You think my daddy hanged himself?" She didn't wait for an answer. "That's what everybody said. They said my momma run off with that salesman, too, but my momma wouldn't do that."

"How old were you when it happened, Maggie?"

"They said I was too young to face the truth, but I wasn't so young I wouldn't know my momma didn't run off and leave me, and my daddy wouldn't hang hisself in that tree like that."

"How old were you, Maggie?" Taylor asked gently.

"Nine. Nine years old. They said I didn't understand nothing, but I knew. We was gonna lose the land, and we knew it, but my momma and daddy was talking about where we'd go. Wherever we went, we was gonna go together. My daddy said that many a-time. My momma loved both of us. She wouldn't a run off with no salesman."

"Why would anyone make up such a story?"

"Whoever killed 'em made it look that way on purpose," Maggie said.

"You believe your father was murdered?" Vanessa asked.

Maggie looked her square in the eyes. "Yes, ma'am, I do. I always said so, but no one listened to me. Everybody said they couldn't believe Tilly O'Malley would do such a thing as running off like that, and wasn't it a shame about poor old Paddy going berserk and killing hisself, but they was all too ready and willing to believe it."

An ancient bitterness invaded her voice. "They was all such good Christian people." She shook her head. "Such fine, God-fearing people. They had to do what was right, yes, ma'am, they did." Anger, galvanized over half a century, flared in her eyes. "They wouldn't let him in the cemetery, did you know that? They didn't put no marker on his grave."

"We went to the cemetery," Vanessa said. "We tried to locate his grave, but we couldn't."

"You went to look for my daddy's grave?"

"Vanessa wanted to," Taylor said.

A pall of silence fell over them as the reality of a man's remains lying buried in an unmarked grave in unhallowed earth filled their thoughts.

"What do you think happened to your parents?" Vanessa asked finally.

"Somebody killed 'em."

"Did they have enemies?"

"No, they didn't have no enemies. Everybody liked 'em. Nobody met my momma that didn't love her and say what a gentle woman she was. And my daddy was a good man. A good neighbor, always ready to lend a hand to someone in need."

"Then why, Maggie? Why would someone have killed them?"

"I don't know," Maggie said, wiping a tear from the edge of her eye with her fingertip. "Could have been a stranger. Somebody just passing through, I guess. Maybe that traveling salesman. Nothing else makes no sense. I don't see as how we'll ever find out now."

Taylor shifted in his chair and leaned forward, propping his elbows on his thighs. "Let's assume, just for the sake of argument, that you're right, Maggie."

Maggie sniffed disdainfully. "Don't have to assume nothing. Just have to believe me when I tell you the God's truth."

"What do you think happened?"

"Either they killed my momma or they carried her off. She was a pretty woman. Everybody said so. I reckon some man might take a fancy to her and carry her off. Maybe that salesman. Maybe he tied her up and carried her off. But if so, then he killed her later."

"Why do you say that?" Vanessa asked.

"'Cause my momma loved me. She wouldn't a left me if she'd had any say 'bout it. If she'd been alive, she'd a come home, no matter what."

"And your father?"

"They knocked him out and hung him in that tree to keep him from talking. He would a fought them to protect my momma. He was Irish. He could fight. But his leg was still bad. So they could a clubbed him on the head."

"Wasn't the death investigated?" Vanessa asked. "Wouldn't the sheriff or whoever investigated it check for bruises?"

"Ha! The sheriff. He didn't look at my daddy once after they got him down out of that tree, even when I told him about the blood. People that's hanged don't bleed like that."

Taylor and Vanessa both came to full attention. "Blood?" Taylor asked.

"Yes, sir. That was the worst part of it. He had blood all over the back of his head and down his shirt."

"And the sheriff didn't check it out?" Vanessa asked incredulously.

"He just said my daddy smelled like a moonshine still, so he probably stumbled down and hit his head his own self. Then he asked me where my momma was and looked in the closet and asked if we had a suitcase. He said that since my momma was gone, and the suitcase was gone, too, that she must've run off."

"How did the salesman enter into the story?"

"Momma had gone into town to the grocer the day before, and when she left, some salesman asked Mr. Fisher—Mr. Fisher owned the store—he asked Mr. Fisher who she was and where did she live and said she was a mighty fine-looking woman. Mr. Fisher remembered that when he heard my momma was gone, and he told the sheriff. The sheriff looked everywhere for that man, but he never did find him."

"That's a pretty flimsy basis for assumption," Vanessa said.

"It was the thirties, and it was a small town," Taylor said.

"Things was simpler to folks back then," Maggie said. "They didn't have so much excitement, no television or nothing. I reckon they liked a good bit of gossip. It didn't matter so much whether it was true, so long as it concerned someone else."

"According to the story, your father had been drinking heavily," Vanessa said. "Could he have gotten drunk and . . . ?"

"He was an Irishman. He bent an elbow now and then. But he wasn't no drunk. And he wouldn't a been drinking in the middle of the day like that. No ma'am.

If he'd a come home from town and thought my momma was gone, he'd a gone after her. He wouldn't a gone to that bottle and got stinking drunk when I was coming home from school in a couple of hours."

Her hands wiped at her skirt again. "And that note, that was another thing. Don't make sense at all that he would get drunk and then write a note. He wasn't much keen on writing even when he was sober."

"He left a suicide note?" Taylor asked.

"The sheriff called it that. I never believed my daddy wrote no note, but he said the handwriting matched the signature on the loan papers at the bank. Old Man Vandover didn't waste no time showing those papers to the sheriff."

"Did you see the note?" Taylor asked.

"No. But the sheriff told me what it said. It said, 'It's too much,' and it had my daddy's name on it."

"'It's too much,'" Vanessa repeated musingly.

"Curiouser and curiouser," Taylor commented.

"I never believed any of it, but no one would listen to me, not even when I begged them to put my daddy in the cemetery. Everybody felt sorry for me. Made 'em feel good to pat my head and show some compassion for poor little Maggie 'cause her momma ran off and her daddy hanged hisself. But nobody would listen to me."

Vanessa laid her hand on Maggie's arm. "It must have been awful for you, losing your parents that way, growing up without them."

"I got on," Maggie said, stiffening her spine.

Vanessa and Taylor exchanged looks that asked, "What next?" Taylor shook his head almost imperceptibly to indicate he was as much at a loss as Vanessa.

Maggie went back to picking at the bow on the potted plant. "You say the tree's still there?"

"Yes," Vanessa replied, relieved to have the dreadful lull in the conversation breached. "It's in my backyard."

"Don't suppose . . ." Maggie said pensively.

"What?" Vanessa asked.

"The flowers wouldn't still be there. It's been too long." She leaned forward and smelled one of the miniature roses, then looked at Vanessa. "My momma loved flowers. Roses were her favorite. She had a bunch of climbing roses near the window, and we used to smell them all summer long."

A tremor crept up Vanessa's spine to tingle her scalp. Roses outside the window, their scents strong and sweet. And a sweet-faced child . . .

She paled visibly, and Taylor put his hand on her shoulder. "Vanessa?"

Instead of answering Taylor, she turned back to Maggie. "Did you—when you were little, did your mother fix your hair in long ringlets?"

Maggie chortled and patted her hair. "Not this hair, no ma'am. Oh, she tried, so I could wear it like the other girls. Momma tried irons, rolling it with rags, everything you could think of. It was like trying to curl hay. Used to put a bowl on my head and cut around it."

Relief flooded through Vanessa. Sheer coincidence and an overactive imagination.

Maggie leaned forward to smell the roses again. "We had honeysuckle on the place, and wisteria, too. In the springtime, Momma used to say our yard smelled like ambrosia. The bees used to just swarm around the vines. Lord, the buzzing was loud as a buzz saw, sometimes."

Vanessa felt as though all the warmth were draining from her body. She rubbed her arms in an effort to fight off the clammy cold pervading them. "Bees," she whispered hoarsely, and turned to Taylor with a stricken expression on her face. "The buzzing noise in the dream was bees."

# 10

TAYLOR STRETCHED his arm across Vanessa's shoulders in a protective gesture as they left the rest home. Vanessa fought the urge to turn into the curl of his shoulder and bury her face in the wall of his chest, knowing that if she did so, she might not be able to stop at that; she might wrap her arms around him and cling to him in a way that would be totally inappropriate in a public place. The warmth and hard strength of his muscles was so reassuring, so seductive, so *safe* that she feared she would lose the last sliver of control she had on her composure and burst into sobs of frustration.

She settled into the passenger seat of the car and stared stoically straight ahead, hands balled into fists as though she could hold on to that tenuous control the way she might hold on to a coin.

Taylor waited until those hands were lying limp in her lap before trying to breach the oppressive silence that had pervaded the automobile. Then he asked simply, "Well? What do you think?"

"From the frying pan into the fire," Vanessa murmured flatly, taking refuge in the old cliché. Then, after a cleansing sigh, she elucidated, "I'm not sure what I think. She was very definite about what she believed, but I don't know how much credence we can attach to any of it."

"Her perceptions did seem very childish," Taylor agreed. "The beautiful, gentle mother and the hard-working, caring father."

"And the unfeeling sheriff," Vanessa said. "She painted him as a villain."

"It must have been hard for her to accept it all."

"Umm," Vanessa agreed. "Obviously she adored her parents. That's normal for a nine-year-old, especially when she loses them so abruptly. It would be difficult for a child to accept that one of them deserted her and the other killed himself."

"You think maybe she refused to see the truth?"

"She might have been incapable of seeing it. How else *could* a nine-year-old cope with something like that? Being abandoned. Suicide. They didn't have the counseling programs they have now. Denial seems a perfectly normal self-defense mechanism."

"And if her mind rejected the truth of how her parents left her life, her memories of what they'd been like might have been distorted."

"You sensed that, too?" Vanessa asked. "That in a childish way she had idealized them?"

"People tend to do that when someone dies—remember them as being finer and nobler and more altruistic than they really were."

"I suppose so," Vanessa said with a sigh. She paused thoughtfully. "I might have given her theories a little more credence if it hadn't been for the sheriff. If there was blood all over the corpse, wouldn't he at least have checked out the cause of death?"

"That's hard to say. It was the thirties, remember? They hadn't seen *Dragnet* and *Quincy* or *Murder, She Wrote*. It probably looked pretty clear-cut to the sheriff. And you know, adults—especially men—didn't pay much attention to children then, either. He would have just seen her as a hysterical little girl."

"Which is her contention," Vanessa said. "That she was the voice of truth and reason, and no one was listening. How do we sort out perception from fact and accuracy from ideals?"

"It would help if it hadn't happened over fifty years ago."

"Do you think there's any chance the sheriff might be alive?"

"Should be fairly easy to find out. There might be files on the investigation, too, if there was one to speak of."

After a thoughtful silence, Vanessa said, "Do you think the adults might have known something Maggie didn't know?"

Taylor shot her an interested look. "Like what?"

Vanessa shrugged. "Who can say? Something they didn't think it was appropriate for a child to know. Something about the salesman, some evidence that Tilly O'Malley had run off with him. Maybe Mrs. O'Malley had a reputation as a flirt, and Maggie wasn't aware of it."

"That's not consistent with the stories we've heard. Every account has been that everyone who knew Tilly O'Malley was shocked when they heard she'd run off. If she'd been a flirt, everyone in town would have known it. And they wouldn't have been so shocked."

"None of the stories have indicated Paddy O'Malley had a problem with the bottle, either. Or that he was the type you'd expect to commit suicide."

"That was the beauty of the legend," Taylor said. "What made the story so dramatic."

"So you don't think it's likely that the sheriff—or all the adults—were keeping something back, hiding it from Maggie to protect her?"

"The kind of details they would have held back are exactly the type of details that make their way into legends."

Vanessa frowned. "Which leaves us with two conflicting accounts and no way to prove either of them." She grew pensively silent. Too quiet.

Concerned, Taylor said, "What are you thinking about so seriously?"

"Bees humming on wisteria and climbing roses next to a window."

"From your dream?"

She nodded. Several seconds ticked by before she asked softly, "How far can coincidence stretch?"

Taylor turned the question over in his mind for a while. "What are you suggesting?"

"I think it's time I did some more research."

They ate dinner at Vanessa's house. Taylor volunteered to wash the dishes since she'd cooked the meal, and Vanessa quickly agreed, then retired to the living room sofa to read the library book on ghostlore. She was totally engrossed in the book when he joined her after finishing the dishes.

"Finding anything?" he asked.

She looked up from her reading. "Nothing reassuring. The isolated facts are beginning to fit together too well."

He sat down next to her. "How?"

"Point one. Traditional ghostlore says that ghosts 'haunt' the area where they were immediately prior to their death. It's usually associated with some trauma related to death, as though they can't quite let go of life because something would be left unresolved. Which could mean O'Malley is still trying to deal with the shock of finding out his wife had deserted him, since he didn't have time to come to terms with it before he died."

"Does that shoot the unhallowed grave theory in the head?" Taylor said.

Vanessa frowned. "Who knows? The rules are so fuzzy. Maybe he's distressed over the grave, but the tree is the only place he's capable of materializing." She looked Taylor in the eye. "Want to hear disturbing ghostlore point two?"

"Shoot."

"Not all returning spirits take humanlike form. Some of them become a gust of cold air. There's an expression when you feel a cool draft creeping up your spine— 'Kissed by a ghost.'"

There was a silence as they both thought about the draft in the corner of the room, the one customer service said wasn't the result of any structural flaws. Vanessa was so serious that her voice was almost a whisper. "Sometimes you smell them."

"Tilly O'Malley grew roses."

"And wisteria. And when Margaret arrived for my housewarming with her roses and wisteria, Karen was standing in that corner. She was almost knocked unconscious by something none of us understood. And that night, Paddy O'Malley showed up in the tree."

She had gained momentum as she stacked the damnable elements into a dreadful possibility. "What if Maggie's right? What if they were both murdered, and I've got two ghosts instead of one? How are we ever going to put either one of them to rest? What if she's in my mind when I sleep, invading my thoughts? What if

I'm reliving her last few minutes of life? Does that mean I'm possessed?"

"No," he assured her, aghast at the fear, at the horror of circumstance that drove her to feel it. He put his arms around her and pulled her close and thought how often since he'd known her that he'd held her just the same way and comforted her. He felt so inadequate pitted against the vast unknown. How did a man protect the woman he loved from the supernatural, from the violence of a crime that might have been committed half a century ago? He tightened his arms around her just a bit, taking solace in the solidity of her body pressed against his. "No," he said, and then murmured the denial one last time before assuring her, "It doesn't mean that."

*Cropville, Texas—1946*

DANNY UNBUTTONED the middle button on the back of Jessica's dress and slid his hand inside. The silken smoothness of her slip, warm from her body, welcomed the caress of his fingertips. He could feel the clasp of her brassiere beneath that thin fabric, and his fingers burned with the urge to undo the metal hooks. Heartened, encouraged, he deepened the kiss with a savage thrust of his tongue into her mouth and inched his hand higher, encountering first the lace edge of the slip and then the velvet softness of her skin. Sexual yearning burst through him with the speed and shocking intensity of a jolt of electricity.

With the same swiftness, Jessica stiffened, gasped, jerked away from him, denying his mouth her mouth, denying his hands the touch of her flesh.

Danny's growl of frustration as he turned his back to her was desperate and feral. His hands knotted into fists, unflexed, knotted, unflexed.

The energy and power he held in check scared her; his vulnerability tore at her heart. "I'm sorry," she said, pitifully close to tears. "I'm so sorry, Danny. I thought it would be different this time."

She succumbed to the sobs threatening to rip open her chest. Again. They'd lost track of the number of times she'd cried, how many times she'd apologized. Danny wiped his hand across the grimace on his face. A tremor claimed his entire body, a brief shudder that betrayed the emotions he was keeping in check.

Several silent, torturous minutes passed before he fortified himself with a sharp intake of air, then said, "We might as well face it, Jessica. Unless we get some help, it'll never be any different."

"Help?" she said. "I...I don't know what you mean."

"Professional help. Doctors."

The color drained from her face. Mortification shone brightly in her eyes. "I couldn't...*tell*...someone. Discuss our most private lives. I just couldn't!"

"Not 'someone,'" he said. "A doctor. A psychiatrist."

"You think I'm crazy!" she said miserably. He tried to put his arm around her, but she shrugged away from him.

"You're not crazy," he said. "But you...we...have a problem."

"Lots of women are nervous at first."

"Nervous, Jessica. Not terrified. Darling, I'm only human. I can't go on like this, wanting you, knowing you're my wife and I can't have you. I'm tauter than a guitar string."

"Do you want to go to—" she choked over her own suggestion "—to one of those women?"

He gripped her forearms and thrust his face close to hers. "No. I don't want another woman, I want you. I want to know my wife the way a man is entitled. *My wife.*"

"I want that, too," she said. "God, I want to be your wife that way. I don't know why I'm afraid. I'm not afraid of you. I love you."

"Don't you see?" he pleaded. "That's exactly what I mean. This fear isn't normal—not this kind of fear, this intensity of fear. A psychiatrist could help you find out why you're afraid, what you're afraid of. I saw them work with battle fatigue cases in the wards."

She jerked away from him violently. "You think I'm crazy. You're trying to have me committed to an asylum. A crazy house." She was beyond logic in her hysteria. "You want control of the bank and the money."

His voice came out like the growl of an angry cat. "The only place I want to commit you to is my bed, Mrs. Bannerson. We've been married three months, and I've never even seen you naked."

She gasped at the sting of his words. "I'm sorry," she said quickly. "I didn't mean to hurt you." Turning away from her, he crashed his fist against the top of the dressing table. "Damn it! How can you say that about your money? I don't care about the money. All I want is you, Jessica. You. A husband has a right to . . . Some men would have taken you by force by now."

"Is that what you want?"

"God, no. There would be no pleasure in it for either of us. But we can't just keep waiting and hoping when nothing is changing, or I'll be the one who ends up in an asylum. We can find a doctor. There's probably one in Houston."

"I can't go to a psychiatrist, a head doctor. You know what everyone would say. There'd be a run on the bank."

"To hell with the goddamned bank!" he shouted.

Jessica was as stunned as she would have been if he had dealt her a physical blow. "The bank is my life!"

"Vanessa. *Vanessa!*"

Her eyes, when she opened them, were unfocused at first, but finally Taylor's face became a clear image as it hovered over hers.

Seeing the recognition, the awareness of time and place register on her face, Taylor lowered himself over her, wrapping his arms around her. The fear lingered with her, and her chest heaved against his as she fought to catch her breath. "It's all right," he whispered. "All right." But he was thinking, *I hate feeling your heart thundering like this when it's not thundering for me.*

Gradually, as her breathing slowed and the thundering abated to a normal life rhythm, he eased his hold on her and finally settled beside her. Her head gravitated to the natural cradle of his shoulder. She closed her eyes and expelled a long sigh. "I thought it was over. I thought she—he—they?—had given up."

More than a week had passed since they'd visited Maggie O'Malley, and this was the first time she'd had the dream. The strain in Vanessa's voice betrayed her desperation and frustration. "I thought our ghost had sensed that we'd gone as far as we could go, that there were no more avenues to explore." She groaned. "There's no place left to find answers for our questions. I thought she was finally going to leave me alone."

Upon learning that the sheriff who'd investigated the death of Paddy O'Malley had been dead for twenty years and that the official files of investigations in the area only went back as far as 1970, they had indeed run out of places to look for answers about what had happened in that farmhouse fifty years before. They were left with nothing beyond the facts that Tilly O'Malley, her suitcase and her clothes had disappeared, and that Paddy O'Malley had been found hanging in the tree, an assumed suicide. Everything else was supposition or theory.

"Was it the same dream as before?" Taylor asked.

"Yes, only more detailed. I see more every time." She rolled her head so she could see his face. "I was screaming in the dream. Was I . . . ?"

"No. You were flopping around like a grounded fish."

"I was trying to get away."

"From what?"

"I still couldn't see it. It was still just a dark shape. Everything else gets clearer and clearer—the scent of the roses, the curtains at the window, the clock bonging, the humming of the bees."

She closed her eyes and burrowed her face against his bare chest. "I knew what they were this time. I didn't wonder what it was. I just heard them, and it registered that it was bees. And the little girl with the long curls and big brown eyes."

Her hand had formed into a fist, and she dealt a gentle blow of frustration to his ribs. "It doesn't make any sense, Taylor. If my mind made her up and put her in the dream after I learned that Paddy O'Malley had a daughter, why didn't it adapt to what Maggie told me about the way she wore her hair?"

"Maybe your mind didn't make her up, after all."

"Okay. Let's throw logic to the wind and assume that I'm not dreaming. Let's assume that I'm watching something like a psychic video of Tilly O'Malley's last few minutes of life. If the little girl isn't Maggie O'Malley, then who is she?"

"A witness," Taylor said gravely.

"If she's..." Vanessa pushed up on one elbow. "What if she's still alive, Taylor? If we found her..."

Taylor raised his hands to cradle her face. "How would we find her? Think, Vanessa. How would we ever find her, even if she is alive? We don't even know who she was."

Exhaling a sigh of disappointment, Vanessa lay back down and said, "You're probably right. There must have been dozens of little girls who wore their hair in long curls. Even Maggie said her mother tried to curl her hair 'like the other girls.'"

There was a silence, then Taylor said, "Marry me."

Overwhelmed by the sudden proposal, Vanessa said his name incredulously.

"I mean it," he said. "I love you, Vanessa. I want you with me. Why should you have to live with something that happened fifty years ago? My house is down there, more than big enough for the two of us. All you have to do is pack your bags."

"I can't just walk away and leave this unresolved."

"You wouldn't just be walking away from something, you'd be walking *to* something. To me. To *us*. To the life we could share."

"You'd never be sure that I wasn't just running away, that you weren't just there with the right offer at the right moment."

"In the end, if you loved me, it wouldn't matter. It would only matter that you were there."

Vanessa's throat closed with emotion. "Do you love me so much that you could take that gamble?"

Taylor laughed unexpectedly. "There's no gamble involved in a sure thing."

She pushed up on her elbow and looked down at him. "How can you be so sure of me when I'm not sure of *anything* anymore?"

Under the cover, he slid his right hand over her ribs, then settled it on her waist and nudged her gently. "Come here and I'll show you."

"Sexual chemistry doesn't prove anything," she said.

"We don't just have sex, Vanessa. We make love."

Vanessa lowered her face to his, letting her arm slide around him as she moved. "Whatever it is we do, I think we should do it now."

"Gladly," Taylor said, tightening his arms around her and insinuating his right leg between hers. His hard, powerful thigh muscles pressed into the sensitive area at the juncture of her legs, and she strained against him, moaning her need deep in her throat as she opened her mouth to his kiss.

His last logical thought before they found oblivion in the pure sensual delight of their lovemaking was that he'd be glad when he could make love to her when she wasn't escaping. He was selfish enough to want her to come to him because she wanted to be with him and not because she was running away from something she didn't understand.

He was somewhat appeased later when, in the after-glow of their lovemaking, as they lay with their naked bodies spooned together, Vanessa's last words before she drifted back to sleep were, "I love you."

# 11

"WHAT ARE YOU LOOKING AT?"

"Your face is four inches away from mine, and you can't figure out what I'm looking at?"

Vanessa smiled. "Okay. I'll rephrase the question. What are you thinking?"

"Besides how beautiful you are this morning and how much I love you and how lucky I am? I'm trying to decide which I love the most—sleeping with you or waking up with you."

"I'm not sure sleep is in the running after last night." She'd had the dream twice and both times woke up terrified.

"I got more sleep here last night than I'm going to get at my house this week, wondering if you're waking up needing me."

Vanessa looked away from him. "We've been all through this, Taylor. It's not as though I'll be alone. Or that I couldn't pick up the phone and call you if I need you. You'll just be at the end of the cul-de-sac."

"Lying awake, staring at the ceiling, worrying about you."

"Karen will be here." Karen's husband was going on a business trip, and Karen, never having lived without parents, roommates or Bob, was nervous about being alone at night. She had asked if she could stay with Vanessa while he was away.

"If you're uncomfortable *cohabiting* with your friend here, then at least explain the situation to her and let me sleep on the sofa while she's staying with you."

"That would be hypocritical. It's not just the co-habiting, Taylor, and you know it. Karen knows I've been seeing you, and she'd hardly expect our relationship to be platonic."

"How a woman who's so beautiful can be so stubborn . . ."

"How a man who's so smart can be so . . . purposefully dense . . ."

"I'm in love. Is that so unforgivable?"

"Well, I think I'm in love, too, but I need . . . You're asking me for a very serious commitment, Taylor—quite possibly the most serious commitment I'll ever have to make, and I can't ground my decisions in fear. This nightmare thing isn't going away. I've got to deal with it before I can think about us. I think a three-day separation—"

"It's not the days I'm worried about," Taylor said. "It's the nights."

"It might be healthy at this point. Don't you see, Taylor? I was perfectly self-sufficient before I met you. I have to find out if I can be self-sufficient again." She touched his face with her fingertips. "Maybe if I discover that in myself, it'll give me the confidence to walk away from this house and its history without feeling like I've left something unresolved."

He trapped her hand and kissed her fingers while his eyes held hers in thrall with the depth of feeling she saw there. "That's the first time you've talked about letting go of it," he said. "If some time and space are what you need in order to resolve this thing in your mind, then

I'll step back and let you have them. Not gladly, but . . . hopefully. Just . . ."

"What?" she prompted when he didn't continue, her voice husky with emotion.

"Nothing." He smiled. "I love you."

"That's not nothing," she said. "It's everything. Tonight will be our last night together for a while. Let's make it special."

"What exactly did you have in mind?"

"A jug of wine, a loaf of bread—and thou. . . ."

"Here-eth, or at a fancy restaurant-eth?"

Vanessa laughed. "Here. I'll even do the shopping."

"I have a contractor coming by after work. It may be seven or so before I get here."

"Good," Vanessa said, sliding her leg over his. "That gives me more time to get everything ready."

"It's going to be a long day," Taylor predicted.

*PAIN SHOT UP HER LEG, and revulsion brought bile to her throat. Buzz. Tick. Bong. The bees. The clock. Her own voice, screaming. The noises blended into a deafening cacophony. She could no longer walk, so she crawled toward the light. She forced herself to look for it, to focus on it. Her heart beat painfully in her chest, and it seemed to her that air wouldn't reach her lungs, no matter how hard she tried to breathe it in. The evil caught up with her. It was inside her. It repulsed her. The light, and in it, a child. She could see the girl's face. . . . Oh, no! No! Please, no . . . !*

A new noise, foreign to the dream, disbelonging, shattered it. Vanessa sprang off the sofa with the last half of a scream still frozen in her throat. Only half-awake, she staggered to the kitchen and picked up the ringing telephone. There was a click, then the dial tone, sounding uncannily like the buzzing bees in her dream.

She put the receiver back in place and held on to it for a moment, drawing support from it while her heart slowed to normal and her mind moved from the past to the present, from nightmare to reality. She hadn't planned on going to sleep when she'd stretched out on the sofa. She'd just meant to rest a few minutes, to shake off the remnants of a trying day at school before she faced the hassle of the supermarket.

The clock on the mantel chimed. Four o'clock. She couldn't have slept more than half an hour. The heaviness that had settled in her limbs made her feel as though it had been much longer. But that heaviness was nothing compared to the fuzziness of her mind. The dream always made her feel that way, disoriented and dull. She covered her face with her hands and groaned. She had to wake up.

Remembering the six-pack of sodas in the refrigerator, she opened the fridge and grabbed a can, then poured the soda over ice. Caffeine on the rocks. If that didn't do the trick, nothing would. She sipped on the cola on her way to the bedroom, then took a long draft before splashing her face with water, combing her hair and changing into comfortable slacks. Then she drained the glass and carried it back to the kitchen.

Refreshed and thoroughly awake, she reached for the running grocery list she kept on a special notepad on the message center next to the phone. Half of the message center was a cork-lined bulletin board, the other half was a slick white surface made to be written on with special erasable markers. She couldn't suppress a smile when she saw the heart Taylor had drawn there. "I—heart—you." He'd signed it T. Just plain T. The intimacy of it thrilled her. Just wait until she told him she'd had the nightmare when he wasn't around and had recovered without hysteria!

The grocery list remained in her purse until she was in the produce aisle of the supermarket, then she pulled it out and read over it. Dish detergent. Cereal. Popcorn, for which Taylor turned out to have a penchant. Routine stuff—except for the last entry.

Taylor must have added it, which was okay. She'd told him to write down anything he needed. But—a jigsaw puzzle? She shook her head in consternation. Leave it to Taylor to do the unexpected!

She thought about it the entire time she was shopping. She wasn't much of a puzzle aficionado, but it might be fun working on a puzzle with Taylor. Okay. So he put a jigsaw puzzle on the grocery list for a romantic evening. So the man was a little...different. He was also madly in love with her. If she hurried, she could run into the toy store at the mall on the way home....

By the time Taylor arrived, freshly showered and shaved, Vanessa had dinner made and candles lit. The puzzle was gift wrapped and waiting for Taylor at his plate.

"What's this?" he asked as they sat down.

"A surprise, for later."

"Interesting rattle," he said as he picked up the box to examine it. He seemed so curious that she would have almost believed he didn't know what it was if she hadn't known good and well that he was the one who'd suggested it.

When he finally did open it, he laughed aloud. "A puzzle?"

"A sexy one," Vanessa pointed out. "It should be very challenging, with all the skin tones."

Taylor, who was studying the two nude torsos depicted on the box cover, gave a distracted "Mm-hmm" of agreement.

Vanessa's stocking-covered toe connected with Taylor's shin under the table. "You know, Taylor, I'd never considered the erotic possibilities in puzzles before."

Taylor grinned at her adoringly. "Is that so?"

"Shocked that I had the guts to buy a puzzle with naked bodies on it?"

"Not shocked, exactly. Surprised."

Vanessa spread her hand, palm down, on his thigh. "It might be kind of *sexy* touching all that skin."

"Umm," Taylor agreed. "But I'd rather touch yours." His hand spread over her thigh.

"I was on my way to the toy store when I saw that crazy party store, you know the one with all the raunchy stuff, and I decided to see if they had puzzles, and voilà, there it was."

"Umm," Taylor said again.

"Shall we clear the table and start working on it now?"

"Now? Tonight?"

"Of course."

"Whatever you want," he said, more compliant than enthusiastic.

"I've never had much patience with puzzles," he said after opening the box to reveal a thousand tiny flesh-colored interlocking pieces.

"I haven't, either," she agreed. "It takes so long to put them together, and I always get manic to finish them." They were sifting through the box, looking for pieces

with straight edges so they could put the border together.

"What made you think of a puzzle?"

Vanessa gave him a perplexed look. "Your note, of
course."

Taylor leaned over and kissed her cheek. "If we both
live to be a hundred, I'll never figure out the way your
mind works."

"What's that supposed to mean?"

"How did you get from a heart on the bulletin board
to a puzzle?"

"A heart?"

"The one on the bulletin board."

"I meant the other one."

An edge of exasperation crept into his voice. "What
are you talking about?"

Irritated by his impatience, Vanessa said, "Did you
or did you not put a jigsaw puzzle on the grocery list,
right under the popcorn?"

"Not!" Taylor said.

"Don't play games with me," Vanessa said, suddenly serious.

"I don't even like puzzles!"

"But . . ." Vanessa said, and then, voice fading, finished, "I don't understand."

"What's this about the grocery list?"

"I was at the store, and there it was at the bottom—
jigsaw. Naturally I assumed—"

"Vanessa, I didn't write anything on the grocery list."

"But it was there. . . ."

"Do you still have it?"

"It's in my purse."

Taylor studied the list for a long time—the everyday
household items were written in Vanessa's plump,

pretty handwriting, each with a single straight line through it. And at the bottom was the word *jigssaw*, misspelled, in a scratchy scrawl.

"Naturally I thought of a jigsaw puzzle," Vanessa said.

"I didn't write this," Taylor said.

Alarmed, Vanessa asked, "Well, I certainly didn't. You can see that the handwriting doesn't come close to matching mine." A pregnant pause passed before she asked, "If you didn't write it and I didn't write it, who did?"

Taylor shrugged helplessly. Vanessa buried her face in her hands and groaned. "Oh, God. The telephone. No one was on the telephone."

"The telephone? When?"

"This afternoon. I fell asleep on the couch, and I had the nightmare, but the phone rang and woke me up. But when I answered it, whoever was on the line hung up."

"Which phone did you answer?"

"The one in the kitchen."

"Next to the bulletin board."

"I didn't—"

"I'm not saying *you* did."

"Ghosts don't write on grocery lists, Taylor."

"Is that a rule?"

"Don't be sarcastic."

"You're the one who told me there weren't any hard-and-fast rules. Who's to say a ghost can't write if provoked?"

Vanessa was speechless. Taylor asked quietly, "Do you still have that book on ghosts?"

"On the coffee table."

While he read, she sat quietly on the sofa, her shoulders lodged against the throw pillows in the corner, her legs extended along its length. "It's not unheard of," Taylor said after snapping the book shut. "Ghosts have been known to move physical objects, close doors, et cetera, so it follows they could move a pen."

"We've all heard of ghostwriters, haven't we?" Vanessa said, bitingly sarcastic.

"It's no more impossible than anything else that's happened," Taylor said. "We have to consider it as a possibility. . . ."

"You want possibilities? I'll give you a possibility," Vanessa said. "How about the possibility that I've gone mad? Let's consider the possibility that I heard the story of O'Malley somewhere and made it all up. And then I heard about Maggie O'Malley and added the child. And now I'm writing cryptic messages on the grocery list. Jigsaw! For heaven's sake! Maybe I'm remembering the time back in high school that we all went to a midnight screening of *The Texas Chainsaw Massacre*."

"Don't do this to yourself," Taylor said.

But she was inconsolable. "Or maybe, somewhere in my subconscious, I just felt like doing a jigsaw puzzle. Now there's an idea!"

"That does it!" Taylor said. Grabbing her wrist firmly, he said, "Come on!"

Vanessa resisted, but he was adamant, and grabbing her other wrist, he carefully pulled her to her feet. "We are getting out of here, away from this house until you come to your senses and quit feeling sorry for yourself."

"Where are we going?" she asked in the car, trying to hold on to her irritation at his bullying when, in fact, she already felt the calming effects of the change of scenery.

"Somewhere frivolous," he said in a tone in direct opposition to frivolity.

Twenty minutes later they were sitting in a booth at an ice cream shop eating sumptuous banana splits. "Feeling better?" he asked.

Vanessa scowled at him. "You can be an overbearing, domineering brute with a caveman mentality when you try." The scowl softened, evolved into a smile. "But you have excellent ideas, and I love you."

"And I love seeing you smile."

They ate in silence awhile, until Vanessa put down her spoon and pinned Taylor with a probing look. "Why *jigsaw*? Is there..." She took a deep breath. "I don't know anything about tools. *Could* a jigsaw be a murder weapon?"

Taylor laughed at the absurdity of it. "Not likely. Jigsaws usually have very small blades. Anyway, it's highly unlikely that anyone could be killed with a jigsaw without bleeding enough to leave undeniable evidence they'd been killed."

Shivering, Vanessa said, "That's a chilling thought." She was thoughtful a minute. "When I saw the word *jigsaw*, I automatically assumed it meant a jigsaw puzzle. Suppose—well, suppose I did write that message. Maybe I used it interchangeably with the word *puzzle*. Maybe it was just my subconscious expressing frustration over the puzzle of a ghost."

"And if Tilly O'Malley wrote it?" he challenged.

"Maybe she was mocking me, daring me to solve the puzzle."

"No," he said. "She needs you. And she's trying desperately to tell you something. There's no telling what kind of energy it might have cost her to write that one word."

"You think her battery's getting low?" Vanessa asked caustically.

Taylor shrugged off the sarcasm. "If it were easy, ghosts would write all the time. She's getting desperate, Vanessa. She must have sensed you were considering leaving. She might even have eavesdropped."

"Why would she bother when she's walking around in my mind, anyway?"

"Vanessa, please. I think she's trying to tell you something very specific."

Vanessa propped her elbows on the table and rested her forehead on her palms. "But what does it mean? Jigsaw?"

"It means that I'm more uncomfortable than ever about leaving you and Karen alone in your house."

"That's tomorrow night," she said, reaching across the table to interlace her fingers with his. "Tonight's still—if not young—just barely middle-aged."

Taylor smiled smugly. "Is that a proposition, Miss Wiggins?"

Vanessa returned the smile. "Come on, Mr. Hotshot Developer. Take me home." As they rose to leave, she said under her breath, "Maybe Tilly will have the puzzle put together by the time we get there."

# 12

FROM THE BEGINNING, Karen's visit took on the character of an old-fashioned slumber party. She and Vanessa rented an outrageously dumb movie their students had recommended, sent out for pizza and sat on the floor Indian-style in their sleep shirts eating and ridiculing the movie and giggling.

"So," Vanessa said during a comparative lull in the silliness, "what's married life really like? Do married people really do it only once a week?"

Karen laughed so hard she choked on her wine but nodded and managed to squeak out between chortles, "No. More often."

"You mean you've had to do it more than once?"

"As if you didn't know."

"Why, whatever do you mean?" Vanessa asked with a perfect Southern belle inflection.

"Don't play innocent with me," Karen said. "I saw the shaving cream in the bathroom, and I want an up-to-the-minute status report on what's going on with the Incredible Hunk."

"Think, Karen. Way back in history, when you and Bob were madly in love . . ."

Karen tossed a throw pillow at her. "I'll get you for that one. Bob and I are *still* madly in love."

"Then you *still* do it?"

"I'm not giving out any secrets until I get some."

They talked until midnight. Then, because they were responsible adults instead of carefree kids, they wrapped the leftover pizza, cleaned up the clutter of their meal and tucked into bed, Vanessa in her own room and Karen in the guest room.

Vanessa spent a few minutes before she went to sleep missing Taylor, thinking about how much a part of her life he'd become, wondering if he was lying awake worrying about her as he'd predicted he would be. Her last waking thought was that, if so, he was worrying needlessly; she couldn't even imagine the possibility of Tilly O'Malley invading her sleep after the frivolous gab session that had just ended.

Never had her judgment been more askew.

ALL THE ELEMENTS were in the dream again: the smell of the roses, the ticking of the clock, the humming of the bees, the menacing presence, the terror, the light, the face. Vanessa saw everything, heard it, smelled it, felt it. She woke up with a scream lodged in her throat, her heart thundering in her chest, her lungs aching for oxygen and Karen standing over her.

"Vanessa?" Karen whispered, almost as though she were afraid to ask.

Vanessa was still trying to gather oxygen into her lungs. "I'm okay," she managed between hurried, gasping breaths. "It was a nightmare."

"I've never heard anyone scream like that," Karen said, sinking onto the edge of the bed. "You scared me out of a year's growth."

They embraced, comforting each other. When they parted, Karen leveled an interrogative gaze on Vanessa. "Has this ever happened before?"

Vanessa rolled her head against the pillow and groaned. "Yes. Oh, Karen, you just don't know...."

"Tell me, then."

"Are you sure you *want* to know?"

"Scoot over," Karen said, nudging Vanessa. When she was seated on the bed atop the covers, she looked down at Vanessa. "When my best friend wakes up screaming like a banshee in the middle of the night, yes, I want to know what's bothering her."

"Oddly enough," Vanessa said, "I think it started with you. No, on second thought, that's wrong. It started with the screaming. Remember when you thought Heather McQueen might have been outside the window?"

Karen nodded.

"That was the beginning. I'm convinced it was related."

"What does it have to do with me?" Karen asked.

"Remember when you were standing in the draft, and you felt...funny?"

Karen shivered. "All too well. It was creepy."

Vanessa sighed. "This sounds so incredible. Karen, I think my draft is a ghost."

Vanessa sensed Karen's skepticism but also her genuine concern as they talked, so she went on, pouring out the story, describing the dream, the visit with Maggie O'Malley, the cryptic entry on the grocery list.

"Jigsaw?" Karen asked, her eyes widening.

"Yes," Vanessa said. "Bizarre, isn't it? It must be a key of some sort, but we can't— What is it?"

"Jigsaw?"

"Yes. Karen, does that mean something to you?"

"No. It's just...Vanessa, that's what you were screaming."

Vanessa pushed up on her elbow. "I was screaming 'jigsaw' in my sleep?"

"Not exactly. Just...something about jigs." Karen paused thoughtfully. "Were you dancing in the dream?"

"No. I told you, my leg was hurt. Why would you think I was dancing?"

"O'Malley. Irish. The jig."

"Jigs.... Jigs." She grabbed Karen's arms. "Karen, it's a name. Jigs. Jigs saw. That's why it was misspelled. It wasn't one word—jigsaw. It was two words—Jigs saw. Jigs is the little girl with the long curls."

"What are you doing?" Karen asked when Vanessa picked up the phone and started dialing.

"I've got to call Taylor."

"At four o'clock in the morning?"

"Taylor would never forgive me if I didn't tell him right away. He's used to it, anyway. It's only fair that I should call him with good news after I've called him with bad news so—"

She snapped to attention and spoke into the receiver. "Taylor? I've got something to tell you. Right. The front door. And Taylor...bring wine. We've solved the riddle. Or at least we're closer to it."

He arrived five minutes later, unshaved and looking adorably disheveled in jeans and a stretched and faded T-shirt that was becoming familiar to Vanessa.

Karen had quickly dashed to pull on a robe when she realized Vanessa's mystery hunk was actually coming over in the middle of the night. She greeted Taylor politely when they were introduced and accepted a glass of wine when he offered it, then listened with all the animation of a zombie while Taylor and Vanessa rejoiced over the breakthrough they were certain they'd made.

"We've got to talk to Maggie again," Vanessa said. "She might remember someone named Jigs."

"Tomorrow," Taylor said.

Vanessa nodded. "I'll call the rest home from school. We'll go as soon as you can get away."

"Hey, you two," Karen interjected tiredly. "I think it's great that you're making some progress with this, but it's four-thirty in the morning, and tomorrow's a school day. I'm hitting the sack."

The click of the guest room door put an end to the silence that followed her exit. Taylor turned to Vanessa and gave her a suggestive grin. "What about you? Want to hit the sack?"

"I'm too keyed up to sleep," Vanessa said.

Taylor leaned over to kiss the wine from her lips and whisper hoarsely, "Sleeping wasn't what I had in mind."

"What did you have in mind?" she asked, wrapping her arms around his neck to keep his face close to hers.

Taylor spread his right arm across her shoulders and slid his left hand under her knees and picked her up. She giggled and tightened her arms around his neck. "Sh," he admonished. "You've got company. It wouldn't be polite to disturb a guest."

"I plan on disturbing you plenty," Vanessa replied, then began nibbling on his earlobe.

"Do you think you could wait until we make it to the bedroom?" he said, straining with the exertion of carrying her.

"Do I get dropped on my great behind if I don't?" Vanessa asked, whispering so Karen wouldn't hear them.

"Quite possibly," he said, huffing and puffing as he maneuvered the corner where the hall made an elbow turn to the right. He groaned with relief seconds later as he tossed her onto the bed, and then he walked back to the door to pull it closed with as soft a click as possible.

He turned back to Vanessa. She had shed her robe and was sitting propped up against the pillows on the bed. His face softened as she cocked her head at a coquettish angle and flashed him a come-hither smile. He moved quickly to the bed to sit down beside her; his hips slid against hers as the mattress slumped in response to their weight.

"May I disturb you now?" she whispered as she moved into his embrace.

"I'm already disturbed," he said. "Soothe me, instead."

VANESSA AWOKE later that morning to the sound of her shower running. She groaned, looked at the clock and rolled over, pulling the covers around her tightly. They were still warm with the heat of Taylor's body, and her groan faded into a sigh.

Minutes later, when she heard him rattling around her vanity, she rolled over and opened her eyes. He was wearing a bath towel wound around his waist, and blotting his wet hair with the matching hand towel. "Sorry about the bathroom," he said. "I didn't want to risk running into Karen in the other one."

"That's okay," she said with a sigh, and realized that it was. He was in her bathroom, and it was perfectly okay.

"I'll go home to shave," he said. "Want me to plug in the coffeepot on my way out?"

"You'll earn a permanent place in my heart if you do."

"I'll make you coffee every morning for the rest of your life if you'll let me," he said, sinking onto the bed next to her. His eyes looked at her face adoringly.

She touched his cheek with her fingertips. "Will you hug me right now?"

"My pleasure," he said as she slid into his arms. They were silent for a moment, then he said, "Anxious about seeing Maggie again?"

Her cheek grazed his shoulder as she nodded. "And hopeful." She sighed heavily. "I want this nightmare to end."

"If there *was* a little girl in Cropville named Jigs, Maggie will remember her," Taylor said.

Vanessa's cheek bobbed against his shoulder again as she nodded silently. Taylor captured her chin in his palm and coaxed her face up so he could kiss her. "Ride to school with Karen in her car. I'll leave work early and pick you up and we'll go directly to the rest home."

"READY TO GO?" he asked as she slid into the passenger seat of his car that afternoon.

"I've been ready since four o'clock this morning. The day *crawled* by. I was a lousy, inattentive teacher. I didn't think three o'clock would ever get here."

Vanessa must have impressed the rest home receptionist with the urgency of their visit when she called for an appointment, because Maggie was already waiting for them in the solarium. She oohed and ahed over the lilac-and-white gloxinia Vanessa had brought her, then, with her usual directness, asked why they'd come to see her again.

She was wearing another shapeless dress similar to the one she'd worn during their previous visit, and her hair hung limply in that artless cut, and Vanessa felt a stab of pity for the little girl with limp, straight hair and a bowl cut who envied all the little girls with curly hair. "Maggie," she said, "last time we talked, you said you thought someone killed your parents, but no one had ever believed you."

"That's right," Maggie snapped.

"Taylor and I believe you." She paused to let Maggie absorb that information, then continued. "I've been having dreams. . . ."

She told an abbreviated version of her dream, softening the nightmare aspect of it. "I think your mother is trying to help us find out what happened, but I need your help."

"I'll help you however I can," Maggie said.

"I want you to think about the little girls you knew around that time. People who lived in Cropville. Was there a little girl named Jigs?"

"Jigs," Maggie repeated the name musingly. "The only one I can think of is Jessica Vandover. Her name was Jessica, but most people called her Jigs."

"Vandover? Wasn't that the banker's name?"

"Old Man Vandover was her daddy."

"Was she a pretty little girl, with big eyes?"

"Yes, ma'am. She was. Just about the prettiest little girl around, always dolled up in fancy dresses, starched and ironed just so. And that hair of hers—it reached almost to her waist. A lot like yours, only longer, and it was curly. She wore it in long curls and always had a ribbon in it in the back."

Vanessa and Taylor exchanged excited, triumphant looks, and Taylor flashed her a thumbs-up. Vanessa turned back to Maggie. "Were you and Jigs friends?"

"Not 'specially. Not friends like would visit or anything. But she knew who I was and I knew who she was,

and we said howdy-do when we saw each other at
school or in town. Some folks thought Jigs was stuck-
up on account of all the money her daddy had and her
being so pretty and all, but I think she was shy. She
weren't never nothing but nice to me."

"Was there any reason she would have been at your
house the day your . . . the day you found your father?"

Maggie thought a moment, then shook her head.
"Not that I can figure. She would a been at school, same
as me."

"Do you know what happened to her, where she is
now?"

"She married some boy after the war and moved off.
I don't recollect as I ever knew where or why. Wasn't
nobody thought she'd ever leave the bank like that.
She'd been running it ever since her daddy died."

Vanessa and Taylor were able to find Jessica Vandover's married name at the bank. The president, who
was two successors removed from her stint of authority, directed them to his predecessor, who remembered
having met her a few times and said his successor had
mentioned her frequently. "He said she had the Midas
touch, like her father. She and that husband of hers
moved off to Houston so he could go to college, and it
wasn't ten years later they had a booming business for
themselves."

"What business was she in?" Vanessa asked, thinking if they couldn't find her through the phone book's
residence pages, they might locate her through the
business pages.

"The nursery business. Started with one little nursery, and now they have a whole chain of them. You
might have heard of them—Banner Nurseries. It was a

word play on Bannerson. That was her husband's name."

They had indeed heard of Banner Nurseries. They were the largest nursery chain in Houston and were quickly spreading into the suburbs to accommodate the owners of the new homes being constructed there. It took only a few phone calls after that to find Jessica Vandover Bannerson.

# 13

"I THOUGHT *I* WAS A PART of your life."

"Oh, Danny, you know you are. But . . ."

"But what, Jessica? But I'm not as important a part? I'm not as important as the bank?"

"That's not true. It's just . . . if people were talking, if they said the bank president was a loony, the bank would fail."

"Then sell the bank. Or hire a manager. You're wealthy apart from the bank, with all your oil wells. We could move to Houston and you could come in and preside over the monthly board meetings."

"Move?"

"Cropville is not the center of the world just because you own a bank here. Did you ever consider that there's not much opportunity for me here?"

She stared at him, dumbfounded. It had never occurred to her that he wasn't happy here, simply because she was.

"Here everyone thinks of me as the bank president's husband," he said. "If we lived in Houston, I could go to college at night, do something in my own right."

Jessica sank into the dressing table chair. "It's all so much. Leaving the bank. Head doctors. Moving. . . ."

He knelt next to her and took her hands in his. "I'm thinking of us, Jessica. You and me. We're married for better or worse. I don't want our lives to be hell. We love each other too much for that."

Throwing her arms around his neck, she burst into fresh sobs. "Oh, Danny, I'm so scared for us. I love you so much."

"Enough? Enough to give up what you've always known and take a chance on something new?"

"I . . . Father would never forgive me if I left the bank."

"It was his bank, Jessica. He chose it. You didn't. He never should have saddled you with it on his deathbed."

"But it's my legacy."

"It's his shrine!" he said bitterly.

"He said as long as I had the bank, I'd be secure. And I'd have prestige."

"You'd always be secure with me, honey. You might not be a big-shot bank president in a one-horse town, but you'd never starve."

"But my father—"

"Is dead, Jessica."

"But he would have wanted—"

"Damn the son of a bitch!"

"You can't talk that way about my father!"

"Oh, no," he said with a sneer. "No one has ever been allowed to talk about Old Man Vandover to his face or yours, have they? But you should hear what they say about him. Maybe you already have. You sound as though you're accustomed to defending him."

"He helped build this town. He helped every farmer in this community at one time or another."

"Is that what you believe or what he wanted you to believe?"

"It's the truth!"

"He was an ornery old bastard who never helped anyone without an ulterior motive—greed."

"Who told you that?"

"No one in particular. Everyone. It's the general consensus when his name is mentioned. Everyone thanks God you're not like him."

"Gossip!" she charged.

"Persistent talk. Persistent gossip usually contains an element of truth. Did your father ever mention all the farms he repossessed during the Depression, especially the year of the bad drought?"

"He was a businessman, not a philanthropist."

"He was a ruthless, greedy opportunist. There was no limit to his greed. He grabbed everything he could legally get his hands on. And then he drilled for oil on it. That's how you got all those fancy oil wells, lady."

She squeezed her eyes shut and put her hands over her ears. "Stop! Please! I can't stand to hear you say those things about him."

"Because you're afraid they're true," he challenged. "You've never been able to face the truth about him, have you? But until you do, there'll be no room for me in your life."

"Please stop," she begged.

"All right," he said with a heavy sigh. "None of it matters, anyway. The only thing that matters now is us."

He hugged her to him and cradled her head in his hands. "Let's get out of Cropville, Jessica. Let's run away and start over. When we get past this problem, we'll have a couple of kids and get a little house with a yard for them to play in. You can dress them in their Sunday best and take them to the monthly board meetings with you."

Trembling, she clung to him. He thought she would never break the silence that bobbed around them like a vast sea waiting to swallow them. When she finally spoke, her words were slow and measured. "Could we plant roses?"

His response was an undignified, surprised, "Huh?"

"Roses," she repeated. "Could we plant roses in that yard and build window boxes for petunias and pansies?"

He laughed aloud and hugged her so enthusiastically that her feet came off the ground. "Baby, I'll build you a greenhouse so you can grow orchids!"

# 14

TAYLOR'S HAND wrapped around Vanessa's. "Are you ready for this?"

Vanessa nodded, just one bob of the head. "Whatever we learn, it's fifty years overdue."

The Bannerson home was a two-story brick house centered on half an acre of treed lawn in one of the most affluent neighborhoods in Houston. Fat white columns and a porch that spanned the front of the house gave it an antebellum South flavor. A white cat sat on the narrow porch, bathing its paws. She regally ignored Taylor and Vanessa's approach.

A young man in his midteens, casually but well dressed in cotton pants and a surfer-style shirt with wide vertical stripes, answered the door. "Oh, sure," he said when they introduced themselves. "Grandmother's expecting you. She's out in the greenhouse. I'll take you."

Jessica Vandover Bannerson was pruning foliage plants and carefully placing the tips she removed in a long tray of vermiculite floating in water. When they entered the greenhouse, she stopped her work.

"These are the people you were expecting," the boy said.

Jessica smiled at the boy. "Thank you, Danny."

"Grandmother!" he said reproachfully.

"Sorry," she said, and corrected herself. "Dan. I keep forgetting."

Appeased, the boy shrugged self-consciously and said, "I'm going back inside."

She followed him with large brown eyes as he walked away, his stride long and graceful. When he was out of earshot, she gave Taylor and Vanessa a wry smile. "Danny was good enough for his grandfather, even after he was a full-grown man and a Marine. Little Danny turns sixteen and suddenly it's *Dan*." Her affection for the boy was glaringly obvious.

Taylor and Vanessa introduced themselves and shook hands with Jessica, who expressed hope that her hands didn't smell like rooting hormones. "Officially I'm retired," she explained, "but I still putter around in here."

She was a handsome woman and doubtless would have been one even if she hadn't been born to affluence, but Vanessa couldn't help comparing the proud set of her shoulders to the droop of Maggie O'Malley's, and Jessica's fashionable khaki slacks and classic plaid shirt to Maggie's shapeless dresses. There was around her eyes, though, those large, expressive brown eyes, a look of vulnerability that paralleled Maggie's.

She had to look up at them, since she was shorter than Vanessa and wearing loafers, and Vanessa was wearing heels. She said, "I believe I know why you've come but, please, tell me how you found me."

"It's rather complicated," Vanessa said.

Jessica suggested they go into the house, where they could be comfortable while they talked. "My husband should be joining us soon. He must have gotten stuck in traffic. Would you like coffee?"

It seemed ingracious to refuse to wait for Danny Bannerson, so they found themselves sitting in the

Bannerson living room while Jessica Bannerson went to the kitchen for coffee.

Taylor reached for Vanessa's hand and gave it a reassuring squeeze. "It's almost over."

"She knows why we're here. If she weren't going to tell us, I think she would have refused to see us."

Danny Bannerson arrived as they were finishing their coffee. He was a stocky man, with a balding pate ringed by gleaming gray hair. He greeted them, shook hands, then sat on the arm of his wife's chair and draped his right arm over the back of it, above her head. Vanessa could see remnants of the proud World War II Marine in the way he sat there, alert and erect, as though prepared to defend his wife if that should become necessary.

Jessica's hair, also gray, was coiffed into an elegant upsweep that framed her face in a flattering way and emphasized her fine bone structure. She looked, at once, as substantial as stone and as fragile as glass. Her chin raised a fraction of an inch as she said, "You were going to tell me how you found me."

"It's going to sound incredible," Vanessa began.

Jessica's shoulders stiffened, and she reached across her husband's thighs to take his left hand in hers. "I'm prepared to hear it."

Vanessa told her about the ghost in the tree, the dreams, the message written in a ghost's hand. Jessica paled and her knuckles turned white from the tight grip she had on her husband's hand, but she nodded to indicate she was listening and that Vanessa should go on.

"When Maggie told us that your nickname was Jigs and that you wore your hair in long curls, we had to find you. Mrs. Bannerson, were you at the O'Malley farm that day?"

The expression on her face told them that she was.

"Can you tell us what happened?" Vanessa pleaded.

Danny Bannerson spoke then, unexpectedly. "You don't have to do this, Jess."

"You're wrong, Danny," Jessica said softly. "I do."

Turning her full attention to Vanessa, she said, "I think I always knew that someday I'd have to tell someone. In a way, I'm almost relieved."

She paused then and seemed to be lost in thought. "You say Maggie O'Malley is still living?"

Vanessa nodded.

"I've wondered about her. She never married?"

Vanessa shook her head.

"What a pity," Jessica said, and then leveled her gaze on Vanessa. "Do you believe in the sins of the father being visited upon the children?" It was a rhetorical question. She sucked in a fortifying breath and said, "In this case, the sins of my father were visited upon the child of another man."

Impatient, Vanessa prompted, "Mrs. Bannerson..."

"I *was* at the O'Malley farm that day," Jessica said. "But before I tell you about it, I'd like to tell you what happened much later." She saw the protest growing on Vanessa's lips and stayed it with a shake of her head. "It's all relevant. You'll know the entire story soon, but I feel I must tell it to you this way in order for you to ... better understand...."

She drew in a deep breath. "I idolized my father. It's important for you to know that. I idolized him the way a child idolizes a parent, especially a little girl her father. My mother died when I was an infant, you see, and he was the only parent I had left."

"He owned the bank," Taylor said.

"Yes. And he made money. Everyone said he had the Midas touch, and I was proud when they said it. I didn't hear a lot of the talk about him and what a heartless money grubber he was, and when I did hear something negative, I tuned it out, because it was inconsistent with the image I had of him. I was proud to take over for him after he died. In some ways I was almost as obsessed with what I perceived to be my position in the community as he was."

She and her husband exchanged meaningful looks after she said this. Her tongue flicked nervously over her lips before she went on with the story. "I met Danny after the war. He wasn't from Cropville. We were pen pals. We'd met through a Write-A-Serviceman morale campaign."

Smiling softly, she looked up at her husband. The sparkle of romance glinted in both their eyes as they recalled the courtship she described. "He came to Cropville to meet me in person and stayed to court me properly. We were very much in love when we got married. I fully expected that we would stay in Cropville forever, running the bank. But Danny wasn't happy there, and there was . . . another problem."

Her chest rose visibly as she sucked in a deep breath, then vibrated as she exhaled it raggedly. "I was very much in love, but there was one aspect of marriage in which I was a total failure."

Bannerson lifted their joined hands to his mouth and kissed the top his wife's hand, then patted it reassuringly. "I wouldn't let Danny consummate the marriage," Jessica said. "I *couldn't*."

She dropped her head, staring at her lap. "It was very humiliating. I was successful at being a bank president, which was very uncommon for a woman in those days. Yet I was a failure as a wife."

Raising her head again, she looked directly at Taylor and Vanessa. "It wasn't just frigidity. It was fear—worse than fear. Terror. It didn't make any sense, because Danny was gentle and patient, and I loved him so much. Finally Danny was able to persuade me to find . . . help."

"That's why you left the bank so abruptly," Vanessa said.

"Going to a psychiatrist wasn't an easy thing for her to do," Bannerson said. "Things were different back then. Men and women didn't even sleep in the same bed in movies, and they certainly didn't discuss their private lives with anyone. For her to go to a doctor and discuss the most intimate aspects of our marriage—"

"I don't see what this has to do with the O'Malleys," Taylor said.

"Oh, but it does," Jessica said. "It has everything to do with the O'Malleys. You see, I was in therapy for months with no improvement. The doctor finally suggested hypnosis as a last resort. He seemed to feel that my terror of sexual consummation was grounded in something in my past."

She swallowed, obviously uncomfortable. "I didn't believe him, of course. I'd grown up pampered, in a very sheltered environment. I knew almost nothing about sex, except that it was something men and women did. I certainly had never had any traumatic sexual experiences."

Her mouth set in a grim line momentarily. "Or so I thought."

A tense silence presided over the room until, finally, she resumed the story. "Under hypnosis I remembered something that had happened when I was ten years old. Something that I had seen at the O'Malley farm."

She paused long enough to catch her breath. "I had gone to school that day, but I had forgotten my homework at home—an essay on springtime. Anyway, I decided to walk home during lunch and get it. Looking back on it, it's hardly likely my teacher would have given me a failing grade for turning it in late, but I had good grades, and I was appalled at the prospect of making a zero.

"I was on my way home when I saw my father's car turning the corner, toward the O'Malley place, and I decided to follow him. It was a warm day and I was getting tired, and I thought he'd drive me to the house to get my paper and then back to school. It didn't dawn on me that it would take me longer to catch up with him than it would just to walk home."

The story was coming out haltingly, as if it were difficult for her to put the painful recollections into words. "I walked and walked, following the direction the car had gone. It seemed like miles and miles, but by the time I realized I'd made an error in judgment and had decided to turn back, I spied the car in front of the O'Malley place. I started running then, thinking I could ask Mrs. O'Malley for a glass of water, and then my father would take me home. But when I got close to the house, I heard . . ."

"Are you sure you want to go on with this?" her husband asked. She nodded that she did, that she would be all right as soon as she regained her composure.

"As I approached the house, I heard someone screaming. A woman. I stopped for a minute, frozen, just listening. Then I decided to sneak up to the house, to see what was happening. I think I thought I could help her, but then I wondered why my father wasn't helping her, because surely he could hear her screaming, too."

Picking up her coffee cup, she looked inside, then drew the cup to her mouth and drained it before replacing it in the saucer. "I went to the window. It wasn't screaming I heard then, it was . . . I didn't know what it was. It was scraping and groaning and what sounded to me like animal-type noises."

An enigmatic smile belied the intensity of the horror she was recalling. "Children were innocent then," she said. "We weren't raised on movies that depict sexual intercourse in graphic detail."

"Your father and Mrs. O'Malley?" Vanessa asked, aghast.

"I didn't understand why he had his pants down. I'd never seen a man naked before, and I was shocked by the size of his organ. I didn't know what he was doing to her, but I understood that he was hurting her when he took her. I'd heard her screams earlier, and she was sobbing. And she was hurt. She was trying to get away from him, but she couldn't. I was so spellbound by what I was watching that I forgot to be careful, and Mrs. O'Malley saw me at the window. She called my name. She was hysterical, of course. I think she was warning me to run away, but I couldn't move."

A dreadful pall ensued, during which no one moved except for Bannerson, who patted his wife's hand slowly. Finally, Jessica spoke again. "My father looked up and saw me. His eyes were . . . maniacal, and I was terrified. He shouted at me to get away from the window. At first I couldn't move, and then he shouted again, to get away from the window. He'd never shouted at me like that, and it scared me even more that he would talk to me that way."

Another silence. "What happened after that?" Vanessa asked.

"I turned and ran as fast as I could. I don't know how far I ran, but I remember having a pain in my side from running so fast for so long. I stopped and looked back then, holding my side, and I saw him coming out of the house, carrying Mrs. O'Malley. She was all limp, and I knew she was dead.

"I didn't know what to do, but I didn't have to decide, because my father drove the car up next to me and told me to get inside. I got into the front seat. I knew Mrs. O'Malley's body was in the back seat, so I was very careful only to look straight ahead. My father drove back to the house, and he made me get out. We went into the bedroom, and he found a suitcase in the closet, and he made me help stuff Mrs. O'Malley's things in it. I remember him opening her drawers and throwing stuff at me. It was all so tattered—I'd always had such nice, frilly underwear, and hers was all ragged and plain."

Jessica paused again, and Vanessa noticed that her knuckles were white because she was gripping Danny Bannerson's hand so tightly.

"We took the personal items off the dresser. She had a hairbrush with a silver handle, and I remember thinking how out of place it was with that ragged underwear. Then we closed the suitcase and carried it outside, and he threw it in the back seat. It made a horrible thud when it landed on Mrs. O'Malley's body."

Her tongue flicked over her lips. "My father drove out into the fields. He seemed to be looking for something. The dust flew up behind the car like a brown cloud. Then he stopped the car, and I saw that we were next to an old well that had been boarded up. He broke some of the boards away and carried Mrs. O'Malley to the well and dropped her down it. He must have broken her neck. There was no blood, but it was awful, the way her head hung all floppy."

She paused again. "He made me carry the suitcase to the well and drop it in before he boarded it up again. Then..." A tear made its way down her cheek. "He took me home and told me to go straight to my room and stay there. I stayed there for hours and hours, trembling...."

She looked at Vanessa and Taylor. "You've got to believe this. I didn't remember any of this until I was hypnotized by my therapist."

They nodded that they believed and understood.

"He came to my room that night. He was quite mad. Even as a child, I knew it, but my mind wouldn't accept it. He talked about what he'd done that day. He wasn't just calm, he was...well, he was elated, as though he'd been to an exciting party or closed a big business deal. He bragged to me about it all. He called Mrs. O'Malley a fool, because he'd offered her a way to keep her farm and she'd said no, but in the end she'd given him what he wanted, anyway."

Jessica was crying in earnest, wiping her tears away with the fingers of her right hand occasionally. "He told me he'd tricked poor Paddy O'Malley into signing a note by telling him that if he signed it, that he would extend his loan instead of taking the farm."

"'It's too much,'" Vanessa thought aloud. "*It's too much,*" she repeated forcefully. Her hand flew to her lips as realization dawned on her, then curled into a fist. "He thought he was extending his loan by putting into writing that the balance was too much to pay. My God! O'Malley thought he was admitting that the loan was too much to pay back and he was signing his own death warrant. Everyone assumed it was a suicide note."

She looked at Jessica, awed. "Your father was a diabolical genius."

Jessica nodded sad agreement. "Unfortunately. After he tricked O'Malley into writing the note, they had a drink to celebrate. My father caught him off guard and bludgeoned him on the back of the head. Once O'Malley was unconscious, all he had to do was hang him in the tree to make it look like suicide."

Bannerson produced a handkerchief from his pocket, and she blotted her eyes and nose. "He turned to me then, and he said that if I ever told anyone what I'd seen or heard he'd do the same thing to me that he did to Mrs. O'Malley. He said I'd be keeping her company in that well."

A sob tore from her throat. "I did better than keep a secret. It was so awful that my mind just blotted it out as though it had never happened. And I didn't remember anything about it, but when Danny wanted to make love to me . . ."

No one moved or spoke for several minutes. Jessica laid her forehead against her husband's ribs, and his arms tightened around her consolingly.

A peculiar numbness pervaded Vanessa's limbs at the horror of the story she'd heard. *A stone thrown in the water*, she thought. All the ripples . . . even fifty years later, there were ripples. One life wasted, another almost destroyed.

"The old well," Taylor asked. "Was it on the O'Malley property?"

"I think so," Jessica said, raising her head. "If it hadn't been, there would have been fences." She swallowed and asked meekly, "Are you going to find her?"

"I'm going to try," Taylor said. "It's time she and her husband had a proper grave."

Jessica nodded mute agreement.

"I'll do everything I can to preserve the privacy and dignity of this situation," he said. "But these things have a way... The press may get hold of it if the authorities get involved, but I'll do all I can...."

She nodded again. "I appreciate that."

There didn't seem to be any gracious way to exit a person's home after opening fifty-year-old wounds, but it was obvious they couldn't just get up and walk out. Vanessa thought of the beautiful teenage boy who'd answered the door. "How many children do you have, Mrs. Bannerson?"

Jessica's smile was proud, the smile of a mother. "Three. All girls. They're all married now, with children of their own. You met Dan. He's our oldest grandson. There are four others, and three granddaughters."

"And you two are still together."

"Over forty years," Bannerson said. "I wouldn't give up a single one of them. The best thing I ever did was go to Cropville to meet my old pen pal."

"You two have built a business empire," Taylor said. "Banner Nurseries. I've bought sod from you for my houses."

"That just happened," Danny Bannerson said.

"I couldn't go back to the bank after walking away so abruptly, but I couldn't just sit at home and do needlepoint, either," Jessica said. "And Danny really didn't have an occupation after he finished college. He'd majored in business. We just looked for something we liked to do so we could work together and enjoy our work, and we were lucky."

The silence this time was comfortable, almost replete. It was time to leave. Vanessa motioned to Taylor and they stood up. She extended her hand to Jessica. "You've been very generous, Mrs. Bannerson. You didn't have to be. I appreciate the fact that you were."

Jessica took Vanessa's hand and looked directly into her eyes. "My therapist and I discussed going to the authorities, but we couldn't see any purpose in it so many years after the fact, especially since my father was long dead. But I think I always knew I'd have to tell someone about it. I'm very glad you came. I feel as though I've taken care of some long-unfinished business."

She turned to Taylor. "If you need help with the grave, the stones, anything, please call on me."

Taylor smiled at Vanessa and draped his arm around her shoulders to give her a squeeze. "I appreciate the offer, Mrs. Bannerson, but I think that little party's going to be on me."

"Call me, then. I'll provide flowers."

"I'll do that," he said. "I'll surely do that."

# 15

THEY WERE SEVERAL MILES from the Bannerson house before Taylor said, "We found out."

Vanessa nodded. Several more minutes passed before she asked, "Do you know of any old water wells on the property?"

"I can make a reasonable guess. I think it's over in the area where they drilled some test holes for oil. There's a slab there—not set into the ground, just set on top of it. We wondered about it when we looked over the area. If the well was there and the boards had rotted, the petroleum crews might have put the slab over it to keep anyone from accidentally stumbling in, or more likely to prevent trucks from driving into it."

"We've got to talk to Maggie," Vanessa said. "She has a right to know."

"Yes."

"What if she wants to be there?"

"Maybe we should talk to Betty Staal first, see if she thinks Maggie's up to it."

"That's an idea."

Maggie surmised that they had news when Betty Staal accompanied them to the home. After hugging Betty and nodding hello to Vanessa and Taylor, she asked with audible trepidation, "You found out something about my momma, didn't you?"

Betty answered, "Yes, Miss Maggie. They did."

Maggie chewed on the information a few seconds, then said, "Well, you folks sit down so we can talk."

There seemed no reason to waste time on preparatory chitchat. Taylor said, "You were right, Maggie. Your mother was murdered. We believe her body is in an old water well. Are you aware of one on the property?"

"That'd be the one that went dry the year before it all happened," Maggie said. "It was out in the far north field."

Taylor nodded to Vanessa to indicate that's where he'd thought it was.

Maggie, sounding almost like the nine-year-old child she'd been when her mother disappeared, asked, "Who killed my momma? Why would somebody do that?"

"It was Old Man Vandover," Taylor said. "He wanted her to . . . give herself to him in exchange for the farm. He got angry when she refused."

At that moment, Vanessa was more certain of her love for Taylor than ever before. His tact had spared Maggie some of her mother's humiliation, and Jessica, too, some of the humiliation of her father's depravity.

"And my daddy?" Maggie persisted.

"Exactly as you thought," Taylor said. "Vandover hit him on the head and then put him in the tree. He tricked him into signing the note, too. Your father thought he was extending the loan at the bank."

A minute or two passed in absolute silence. Maggie cried, but quietly, without sobs, and the tears slid noiselessly down her cheeks. Tears of pain. And gratitude. Tears of release, because now she knew the truth.

"I knew she was dead all along," she said at length. "If she'd been alive, she'd a come back for me."

"What do you want to do?" Taylor asked. "The choice is yours—we can leave her there, or we can try to find her and bury her next to your father?"

Maggie's eyes widened. "Side by side? In hallowed ground? With a proper stone?"

Taylor nodded to all of it, and by fractions of an inch, a smile crept over Maggie's face.

"YES, SIR. This is where the well was, all right," Maggie said.

They were in the still-undeveloped quadrant of the O'Malley property. Taylor turned to Burleigh, who'd agreed to give him a hand removing the slab. "Let's get it uncovered."

The concrete slab cracked and rent as it was moved, and they had to haul it away in segments, using heavy wire run through a winch and pulley mounted in the bed of a Stephensco construction truck. Any protrusion of well wall had been shorn away before the slab was put in place, and what they eventually uncovered was a menacing-looking dark hole about three and a half feet in diameter.

Vanessa's scalp prickled when she looked down into it, although whether it was from knowing what might lie at the bottom of that blackness or simply that the dark chasm seemed somehow macabre in its own right, she wasn't sure.

Maggie seemed to think that the well had been about thirty feet deep. Taylor had brought fifty feet of rope, which he'd marked in five-feet increments. To this he attached a heavy, battery-powered lantern.

"Be careful," Vanessa warned as he stepped to the edge of the hole and began lowering the lantern.

Taylor gave her an exasperated scowl. "Yes, Mother."

"Sorry," she said. "I just—"

"It's not the first time I've worked around a hole in the ground, Vanessa. It won't be the last. I hope you're not going to turn out to be a nag." He was grinning so endearingly that she answered him with an exasperated smile.

Betty had urged Maggie to sit down in one of the lawn chairs Taylor had opened and placed in the stingy shade of a nearby mesquite tree. Vanessa knew she should join them, but the well fascinated her. She peered over the rim, watching the slow journey of the light until it was so deep that the darkness above it rendered it ineffectual. Then there was nothing else to do but wait until the lantern reached something solid and the tension on the rope turned to slack.

"Twenty-nine feet," Taylor announced when, after jiggling, the rope remained slack.

They stood at the edge—Taylor, Vanessa, Burleigh—and stared at each other.

"What now?" Vanessa asked.

"The fire department has a special team trained for this sort of thing, but I'm not sure we can get them out here simply because we found a well. We'd have a lot of explaining to do. If we had the suitcase—"

"What suitcase?" Burleigh asked.

"We have reason to believe that a woman's body was thrown in this well fifty years ago," Taylor said. "Her body and a suitcase with all her things in it."

"I'm not cotton to touching any bodies," Burleigh said. "But if there's a suitcase down there, why don't you lower me and let me get it?"

"It's too small," Vanessa said, aghast at the idea.

"Hell," Burleigh replied, "I crawled through tighter pipes than that in the army."

"The walls could be unstable," Taylor said.

"They looked sound as far as we could see. But I'm nobody's hero and nobody's fool. First sign of crumbling around my feet, and I'm out of there. You'll be hearing me holler to get my arse up."

"You wouldn't have much room to maneuver," Taylor said.

"I'll bring it up with my feet if I have to."

They discussed it another ten minutes before Taylor was convinced, and he and Burleigh began fashioning a harness. The next half hour was probably the longest waking half hour of Vanessa's life. Inch by inch Burleigh disappeared, and there was nothing left to see then except the taut line centered over the hole and the light disappearing into the bowels of the well along with Burleigh.

Vanessa's anxiety was mirrored in the grave set of Taylor's jaw, but if Burleigh shared that anxiety, he didn't show it. From inside the well, they could hear him singing "Ninety-nine Bottles of Beer on the Wall."

He was down to the eighty-ninth bottle when he called for them to quit lowering. The next two minutes were interminable.

Sensing the tension, Maggie and Betty walked to within hearing distance of the well. Along with Taylor and Vanessa, they heard Burleigh's very pronounced, "Haul me up."

Collectively they held their breaths while Burleigh worked from the eighty-eighth bottle to the eightieth, and then Taylor was helping a very dusty Burleigh out of the well. "This what you're looking for?" he asked. Wedged between his feet, covered with filth but clearly identifiable by its shape and size, was a suitcase.

Suddenly the center of attention shifted to Maggie as she walked slowly to the spot where the case had landed and gingerly, as though she were afraid it might disintegrate, worked at the catches. In the end, Taylor pried them open with his pocketknife. Maggie gasped as the decaying remains of her mother's clothes and personal items fell open to view. Her chin quivered as she stared at them for a moment, and she wept when she picked up her mother's hairbrush and held it in her hand.

Feeling the warm flow of tears on her own cheeks, Vanessa was grateful when Taylor draped his arm around her shoulders and gave her a reassuring hug.

Taylor called his friend in the sheriff's department, who took one look at the suitcase and called in the fire department special rescue unit. Vanessa sensed that the sheriff's deputy knew he was being told half a story, but since the body obviously had been in the well for many years, and the identification, through the personal items in the suitcase, was so positive, he did not push for details he might have in a more current crime situation. He did not insist on knowing, for instance, why Maggie fortuitously happened to be there when the suitcase was discovered or why Burleigh had felt the compulsion to lower himself into a possibly unstable well that had been capped by a concrete slab for nigh onto fifty years.

What was left of Tilly O'Malley's body—bones and a scrap of faded cotton print—was brought up and given the dignified covering of an official body bag, then transported to the county morgue in an ambulance.

The ambulance pleased Maggie. And the official process eventually provided them with a death certificate, which made it easier to arrange for a formal burial site and provided reasonable grounds for having the body of Paddy O'Malley exhumed so his grave could be relocated. One interesting note on the autopsy was the opinion that Tilly O'Malley's right leg had been broken immediately prior to her death.

A small article appeared in the pages of the local paper, but it mentioned only that a body had been found, raised from the well by paramedics and identified as belonging to a woman who'd resided in the area and disappeared in the 1930s.

"You are a genius," Vanessa told Taylor as they lay in her bed, and kissed him appreciatively. "I can't believe the way it's all working out."

"Excited about next week?" he asked.

She nodded. "Aren't you?"

"It'll be my first Irish wake," he said.

The following Sunday afternoon they stood at the foot of a double grave in a beautifully kept local cemetery, while a priest in full raiment conducted the proper services over the graves. The headstone, etched with an oak-leaf-and-roses motif, held the name O'Malley in large letters, and under it, side by side, just as the caskets now lay under the earth, the names Tilly and Paddy, with their birth dates and the date of their deaths.

After all that had happened, Tilly O'Malley's birthdate had been the biggest surprise of all, for it was perhaps the most intimate thing she and Vanessa shared. They'd both been born on the sixth of November. And Tilly had been, at the time of her death, exactly the age Vanessa would reach on her next birthday.

*Kindred spirits.* If the idea gave Vanessa an eerie feeling when she let her mind dwell on it too long, it also deepened her sense of satisfaction in seeing Tilly and Paddy O'Malley properly interred.

The wake, like the burial, was unconventional, since it started after the funeral, but there was nothing conventional about the situation. The wake was held at Vanessa's house, and Maggie, the guest of honor, wearing a cornflower-blue dress acquired during a marathon shopping trip to the mall with Betty Staal, walked the length and breadth of Vanessa's yard, admiring the roses Vanessa had planted and examining the fledgling wisteria vines Margaret had given Vanessa. Inside she explored the house with interest, exclaiming over the synthetic marble vanities, walk-in closets and automatic dishwasher.

Burleigh had come, too, at Maggie's insistence, but Vanessa suspected he was celebrating the substantial bonus he'd found in his pay envelope as much as the relocation of Tilly O'Malley's body—a bonus destined to be doubled at Christmastime due to the generosity of Jessica Vandover Bannerson, who would be identified to him only as an anonymous benefactor.

Vanessa had prepared a dinner buffet with ham, candied yams, black-eyed peas and corn bread. Taylor surprised everyone with Irish whiskey and a set of ornate shot glasses for an after-dinner toast to eternal peace for Maggie's parents.

After the toast was made and drunk, Vanessa went to the kitchen to put on coffee to serve with dessert. Betty had brought a cake, Karen, a pie.

Maggie walked to the back window and stared out at the oak tree. It was not the first time she had done so.

Vanessa mentioned it to Taylor in the kitchen. "I've done the same thing during the past week," she said.

"Looked out that window as if I might suddenly see the two of them standing there under that limb waving at me."

"That's contrary to all ghostlore," Taylor said.

"I know. It's just my preoccupation with their story. I'm not really expecting to see them at all. It's a wonderful feeling to look out there and think something like that without that pervading fear that I'll *actually* see a ghost."

Taylor stepped behind her and put his hands on her shoulders. She felt the warmth radiating from his body, a seductive warmth that drew her to him. She let her shoulders relax against his chest. "It's over now," he said.

"I know."

"It's time for us."

She turned into his embrace. "I know that, too."

"No lingering doubts about my loving you?"

She smiled up at him. "No."

"No doubts about loving me?"

Raising onto tiptoes, she kissed his mouth briefly. "Absolutely not. I just . . . It's going to take some time. Among other things, I have to decide what to do about the house."

They turned at the sound of someone entering the kitchen. "Excuse me," Jessica said, embarrassed to have caught them at an obviously intimate moment. "Vanessa, I was wondering if it might be possible to speak with you privately a moment."

"Of course." She turned to Taylor. "You can manage the coffeepot, can't you?"

# Epilogue

A PIERCING SCREAM rent the air. Vanessa jerked awake. "Taylor?"

He was standing at the window, peering through the open blinds at the peahen perched on the limb of the huge oak tree outside their second-story window. He turned to her and smiled. "Sound very human, don't they?"

"Too human for comfort," she agreed.

Taylor walked to the bed and sat on the edge. Lifting the covers, he said, "Scoot over, Mrs. Stephenson."

She cuddled into his arms, wove her bare leg between his and sighed. "Except for those stupid peacocks, this place is perfect. I could stay here, just like this, forever."

"Umm," Taylor agreed.

Vanessa turned her face toward his on the pillow. "I'm glad we did it this way. I'm glad we moved everything but left all the boxes packed until we got back so that I could unpack them as *Mrs.* Stephenson. I'll feel much more comfortable finding places for them knowing that your house is officially *our* house."

"I like the sound of that," Taylor said. He kissed her. "I love you, Mrs. Stephenson."

"It was strange, packing up everything so soon after I'd moved there. When I moved into that house and signed that thirty-year mortgage, I half expected to live there for the rest of my life."

Taylor hugged her tighter against him. "No commuter marriages in this union."

"Oh, I agree, Mr. Stephenson," Vanessa said, and sighed contentedly. "No regrets on my part." After a thoughtful pause, she said, "Do you think Maggie will be happy there?"

Taylor laughed. "If the way she and Jessica scoured every inch of the yard discussing landscaping and potential garden plots is any indication, I'd say she's going to be deliriously happy."

"She seemed content with the idea of being there."

"She felt at home."

"Yes. I don't know why I didn't see it immediately. It was so obvious. But I nearly fainted when Jessica asked if I'd consider selling the house to her so she could let Maggie live there."

"It worked out well for everyone," Taylor said.

"As well as it could," Vanessa agreed.

They fell silent, utterly comfortable with each other. Then, after a long, reflective moment of quiet, Vanessa said, "It seems so unreal now, so incredible. Like a dream."

"It always will," Taylor predicted.

"If you hadn't been there—"

"But I was," Taylor said. "And if there hadn't been a ghost, I'd have been there, anyway."

"Are you sure of that?"

"All I have to do is watch you walk across the room and I'm positive of it."

"Ah, yes, my finest feature follows me wherever I go."

"I like your eyes, too, Mrs. Stephenson. I love the way you look at me."

"What else do you like?" she challenged.

"Your hair," he said. "And your nose and your smile and your lips. You've got great lips."

"The better to kiss you with," she said, and did just that.

This month's
irresistible novels from

# —TEMPTATION—

## MONTANA MAN by Barbara Delinsky

Picking up a hitchhiker in a blizzard was a dangerous thing to do, but Lily Danziger was already living on the edge. She was running away, destination unknown. Perhaps this rugged stranger would provide the shelter she needed.

## DARK SECRETS by Glenda Sanders

When Vanessa Wiggins first reported screams coming from behind her home, Taylor Stephenson dismissed her concerns. He convinced her no one had been murdered; no body had been found. And then the ghost appeared . . .

## TO BUY A GROOM by Rita Clay Estrada

Sable LaCroix paid Joe Lombardi to marry her. She desperately needed a complete family to keep her son. It was the perfect business arrangement on paper – unfortunately she hadn't considered her desire to be Joe's wife in *more* than name only.

## GLORY DAYS by Marilynne Rudick

Ashby and her husband, Brian, shared a dream – to win the Olympic marathon. Only their passion for each other rivalled their passion for running. Training together, they were an unbeatable team – until Brian was injured. And then Roger Atlee, rumoured to take a very *personal* interest in his women, began to coach Ashby.

Spoil yourself next month
with these four novels from

## —TEMPTATION—

### JUST JAKE by Shirley Larson

Alexandra Holden was on the verge of success selling her property in the Florida Keys. All she had to do was evict the sexy and distracting Jake Hustead . . .

### TEMPERATURE'S RISING by Susan Gayle

Nurse Kyla Bradford knew Ted Spencer wasn't sick the moment she encountered him. He was trying to fake his way into Emergency to get the scoop on the hospital's latest controversy. She would have to teach him a lesson.

### CHEAP THRILLS by Tiffany White

He was no Peeping Tom: Crew Harper was just doing his job – outside the fourth storey of an office block. But a movement through the window caught his eye – Alexia Grant was undressing!

### THE MAGIC TOUCH by Roseanne Williams

When Brenna Deveney signed on as relief veterinarian for the injured and bedridden Dr Trip Hart, she had no idea she would be tending the sexy bachelor along with the other animals.

# Life and death drama in this gripping new novel of passion and suspense

Following a vicious attack on a tough property developer and his beautiful wife, eminent surgeon David Compton fought fiercely to save both lives, little knowing just how deeply he would become involved in a complex web of deadly revenge. Ginette Irving, the cool and practical theatre sister, was an enigma to David, but could he risk an affair with the worrying threat to his career and now the sinister attempts on his life?

## W⦿RLDWIDE

Price: £3.99    Published: May.1991

Available from Boots, Martins, John Menzies, W.H. Smith, Woolworths and other paperback stockists.
Also available from Mills and Boon Reader Service, P.O. Box 236, Thornton Road, Croydon, Surrey CR9 3RU